"You really get to me. You know that, don't you?"

She straightened enough to be able to see his face, with eyes that had never been so blue. "Because you feel sorry for me?"

"Angry for you," he corrected. "You're a strong woman." His jaw flexed. "A beautiful woman. And I shouldn't even have said that."

"Why not?"

"As much as I want to kiss you, I need you to be able to trust me more." He made a sound in his throat. "Which means I should get my hands off you."

His arms tightened instead, for only an instant. Feeling his arousal, heat settled low in her belly.

"I like your hands on me," she admitted.

He groaned. "I'm trying to behave myself."

She ached to feel his mouth on hers, but how could she initiate anything when she still had secrets? Still, she gripped his shirt in both hands, unable to look away from him.

His head bent slowly, so slowly she knew he was giving her time to retreat. Instead, she pushed herself up on tiptoe to meet him.

WITHIN RANGE

———

USA TODAY Bestselling Author

JANICE KAY JOHNSON

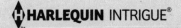
HARLEQUIN INTRIGUE®

Recycling programs
for this product may
not exist in your area.

ISBN-13: 978-1-335-64090-1

Within Range

Copyright © 2019 by Janice Kay Johnson

Printed in U.S.A.

HARLEQUIN®
www.Harlequin.com

An author of more than ninety books for children and adults with more than seventy-five for Harlequin, **Janice Kay Johnson** writes about love and family, and pens books of gripping romantic suspense. A *USA TODAY* bestselling author and an eight-time finalist for the Romance Writers of America RITA® Award, she won a RITA® Award in 2008. A former librarian, Janice raised two daughters in a small town north of Seattle, Washington.

Books by Janice Kay Johnson

Harlequin Intrigue

Hide the Child
Trusting the Sheriff
Within Range

Harlequin Superromance

A Hometown Boy
Anything for Her
Where It May Lead
From This Day On
One Frosty Night
More Than Neighbors
Because of a Girl
A Mother's Claim
Plain Refuge
Her Amish Protectors
The Hero's Redemption
Back Against the Wall

Brothers, Strangers

The Closer He Gets
The Baby He Wanted

The Mysteries of Angel Butte

Bringing Maddie Home
Everywhere She Goes
All a Man Is
Cop by Her Side
This Good Man

Visit the Author Profile page at Harlequin.com.

CAST OF CHARACTERS

Helen Boyd—A single mother, Helen has been on the run for over two years. She almost feels safe in Lookout...until she finds a dead woman in her kitchen, and a police detective becomes entirely too interested in her.

Seth Renner—Detective Renner knows a lie when he hears one...and he recognizes fear, too. Is there any chance the killer murdered the wrong woman? And though Seth can't trust Helen, why is he dangerously tempted by her?

Jacob Boyd—A two-year-old charmer, he gets really anxious when his mom leaves him even for a few minutes. And why not? He has no one else.

Andrea Sloan—She's barely a casual acquaintance of Helen's, so why is she in Helen's house, uninvited...and dead?

Richard Winstead—Finding out he has a son he didn't know about enrages Richard. Divorce was one thing; hiding his child from him another.

Michael Renner—A retired police officer and Seth's father, Michael trusts his son's judgment enough to lay his life on the line for the woman and small boy he suspects his son loves.

Allie Hollis—Desperate for something only her sister can give her, Allie accepts that it may never happen.

Chapter One

"Birdie!"

Helen Boyd glanced in the rearview mirror first to her two-year-old son, then out the side window to the row of crows sitting on the electrical wire.

"Lots of birds," she agreed. "Those are crows. Crows are always black." Helen had the passing thought that in some cultures, they were considered bad luck. Or was that ravens?

Jacob tried to shape the word, which came out sounding more like "cow."

"Crow," she repeated. "Like 'row, row, row your boat,' only it's *c-row*."

He giggled. "K-k-krow."

"Yes." She laughed. "And we're home!" Thank heavens; her feet were killing her, and she was starved. The day had been so busy, she'd never had a chance to stop for lunch. And, ugh, this was only Tuesday.

Home was a small rental house with an

even smaller detached garage that held the lawn mower, a rolling tool chest belonging to the landlord, and some boxes and furniture that might have been left by previous tenants. There was no room for a car, so she parked in the driveway.

Helen climbed out stiffly, her attention caught for a brief moment by bright sails on the Columbia River. Her view was barely a sliver, but that was better than nothing. This was June, but the day seemed way too chilly for anyone to want to go windsailing. Whoever was out there was sure dedicated to the sport, she'd learned. The winds channeled through the Columbia Gorge were one of the biggest draws of the small towns strung along the banks of the river east of Portland.

She circled around to release Jacob from his car seat and swing him up in her arms, using her hip to bump the door closed. "Hamburgers for dinner tonight," she told him.

"Hot dogs!" he shouted.

She planted a big kiss on top of his head. "Hamburgers."

He loved to argue. "Hot dogs."

"Hamburgers." After letting them in the front door, she set him down, staying crouched beside him for a minute. "Do you have to go potty?" He still wore a diaper at night but was doing pretty well using the toilet during the day.

"Uh-*uh*," he declared.

"Hmm." Tempted to kick off her heels right now, Helen decided to make it to the bedroom first. Set a good example. Or maybe she should dump them straight in the trash. There was a good reason they'd been on clearance. Knowing Jacob would follow her, she started for the hall—and came to an abrupt stop, staring into the kitchen.

What on earth was that?

Her heart thudded hard. Jacob, fortunately, was clambering up onto the sofa. She took a tentative step, then another, disbelief and fear clawing inside her chest.

It was a high-heeled shoe sitting all by itself that had first puzzled her. She had *on* the only pair of black pumps she owned. But then… then she saw the woman who lay sprawled on the kitchen floor.

Fingers pressed to her mouth, Helen tiptoed closer. Dark hair fanned over the lifeless face, but Helen could see enough…including the hideous dent in the woman's head.

"Oh, no, oh, no." Helen backed away.

From just behind her, Jacob said, "Mommy?"

Whirling, Helen snatched him up and pressed his face to her shoulder. Then she ran for the front door, pausing only to grab her purse on the way.

"THAT THE HOMEOWNER?" Detective Seth Renner glanced toward the car parked somewhat crookedly at the curb in front of the house.

The uniformed officer followed his gaze. "Don't know if she owns it or rents, but that's her. Name's Helen Boyd. She's got a two-year-old in the car."

Easy to imagine how quickly she'd fled the house when she discovered a dead woman on her kitchen floor. Unless, of course, she'd had something to do with the death, but he wasn't ready to speculate yet.

Instead, he signed the log the responding officer had started, bent to put on disposable shoe covers and stepped into the house. Scanning the living room, he saw evidence that a toddler lived here: a small plastic wagon piled with building blocks, a tidy pile of simple wooden puzzles on the fireplace hearth and a crib-size comforter crumpled at one end of the sofa. Built-in shelving to each side of the fireplace held books, including a good-size collection of children's picture books. Coffee table with rounded edges. Foam had been fitted to cover the sharp edges of the brick hearth. TV. If not for the books, the room would have been stark.

Because there was no art, he realized. Maybe this was a rental, and the woman didn't feel like she could put holes in the walls. Although, he'd have expected to see framed photos or something decorative on the mantel.

He shook his head slightly and moved on to the kitchen, pausing in the doorway to study the body and then work outward to the surroundings.

No indication of a struggle. His first guess was that the victim had been in the kitchen, heard something and started to turn, only to be stunned by the single blow. Dead from that moment, she'd dropped to the floor. Finally going forward to crouch beside her, he did note a dirty mark on her white blouse. It didn't go with her businesslike attire: fitted blouse, blazer, black pencil skirt, heels and hose. A shiny black handbag sat on the small kitchen table, a smartphone beside it. Had the killer kicked her once she was down?

He snapped on latex gloves and gingerly reached in the handbag for a wallet, opening it to see the license in a clear plastic sleeve. Photo looked like a match to him. Seth studied it. Andrea Sloan, brown hair, brown eyes, five foot six, thirty-six years old, organ donor.

Too late for that.

He let the wallet fall back into the purse, looking instead at the woman's face, slack in death.

Why had Andrea Sloan been killed? And why *here*, in another woman's house? Unless she was a close friend, sister, something like that to the owner-renter who'd discovered her?

Still gazing down at the body, he called for a crime scene unit from the Oregon State Police, then walked through the rest of the house. It was immaculately clean and uncluttered. Apparently, the kid didn't go to bed without putting away his toys, and Mom or Dad—was there a dad?—didn't toss dirty clothes over the single chair in the slightly larger bedroom that held a full-size bed, bedside table with a lamp and clock, and a dresser. No art here, either, no photos. Curious, he nudged open the sliding closet door to find it less than a third full. Several pairs of shoes lined up in a neat row on the floor, some unexciting dresses, blazers, skirts and slacks on hangers. Nothing that appeared to belong to a man.

The bathroom was shared with the kid. Nothing suggested a man lived here, either. A toothbrush holder and two toothbrushes sat alone on an otherwise pristine counter.

Pretty clearly, the residents consisted of a single mother and child.

Time to talk to the woman.

Going back outside, he shed the shoe covers and followed the narrow concrete walkway to the sidewalk and the car, a Ford Focus he guessed to be at least ten years old, possibly a lot more than that. He opened the front passenger-side door and bent to look in.

"Ms. Boyd? I'm Detective Seth Renner. I need to talk to you. Is there someplace—" A small boy poked his head between the seats.

"Boo!"

Seth pretended to jump, suppressing a grin. "And who are you?"

"I'm Jacob," the boy declared. He had an impish face, a scattering of freckles across his nose and russet-red hair.

"It's good to meet you, Jake."

"Jacob."

"Ah." Seth focused on the woman again, taking in her appearance and noticing she had more than a passing resemblance to the dead woman. Although if they were related, wouldn't Ms. Boyd have said so?

"Is there someone who can watch Jacob for a few minutes?"

"I... Yes. If she's home, my neighbor is usually willing. Let me—" She jumped out, slammed her door and hurried around to his side, letting him see that she was five foot six or seven, long-legged, thinner than he suspected she was meant to be. When he backed away from the opening, she took his place.

"Jacob, honey, let's go see Iris."

"I like Iris," he stated in apparent delight.

Seth had noted the movement behind the front window of the house next door. In fact, he intended to interview whoever lived there next. He strolled behind Ms. Boyd, who carried the boy on her hip. The front door opened even before they reached the small porch, revealing an elderly woman with deep wrinkles and a warm smile for the little boy.

Ms. Boyd explained briefly that she'd arrived at home and somebody had gotten into her house. She needed to talk to the detective. "Could you…?"

"Of course I can!" Iris cast a worried look at Ms. Boyd but beamed at Jacob. "I just baked chocolate chip cookies. Would you like one, Jacob?"

He held up his hand with all five fingers splayed. Iris laughed and took the boy's hand. The door closed.

Surely at his age the kid couldn't count. He

obviously got the concept that more fingers represented more cookies, though.

For just a minute, Ms. Boyd stayed where she was, looking as if she'd give almost anything to follow her son inside. But finally her shoulders squared and she turned.

"Do we have to go in my house?"

"No," he said. "Why don't we sit in your car?"

Relief seemed to loosen some of the fear he'd seen on her face. Her teeth closed on her lower lip and she nodded. "Yes. Okay."

He let her get into the driver's seat again, guessing she'd feel more comfortable there, more in control. He had to move the passenger seat way back to accommodate his long legs, which meant she had to twist a little to look directly at him.

"Detective…? I'm sorry, I know you introduced yourself, but—" Her voice trembled.

"Renner."

Her eyes fastened on his. "I'm sorry. It's just—"

"You're understandably upset." He watched her closely while trying to appear relaxed and even friendly. "Tell me about your day. Anything out of the ordinary?"

"Not until I got home. The rest of the day… Do you care?"

"I'd like to hear about it."

"I commute to Portland every day. I work as an executive assistant."

He took a notebook from an inside pocket and jotted down the name of the company, her boss and the phone number.

"I left at 5:30. I'm pretty insistent on that, since I have to pick up Jacob from day care by 6:00."

That sounded standard to him. He made a note about the day care, too, an in-home one.

"I parked in the driveway, like I always do."

He left the question of why she didn't use the garage for another time. She sounded steady enough now to make him curious. Anxiety wouldn't have surprised him; her poise did.

"I carried Jacob in," she continued, "set him down and started toward the bedroom."

"Just like that?"

She stared at Seth. "I told him we were having hamburgers, and he insisted he wanted hot dogs. Oh, and that he didn't need to use the potty. Is any of that relevant?"

He smiled. "No, you sound like you were rushing."

"Well, I was, because my feet hurt." She glanced down. "They still hurt."

He saw that she wore black pumps. "They look similar to the shoes the victim was wearing."

No, her outfit didn't match, but color-wise… yeah. Almost. A cream-colored, finely knit cardigan over a sleeveless top, and black dress pants. If someone had seen her go out the door, then caught sight of this Andrea Sloan in the kitchen, a mistake might be possible.

Seth reminded himself not to jump to conclusions.

Ms. Boyd swallowed. "I know. There was a weird minute—"

A weird moment?

Shaking her head, she said, "I just thought, did I leave my shoes in the middle of the kitchen floor? But they were still on my feet, so that didn't make sense, and I'd already seen the…her legs. But…my mind wasn't making the connection right."

"That's often the case when you see something completely unexpected," he said gently.

She shuddered. "Yes. I took a step closer, and then realized Jacob was coming into the kitchen after me, so I grabbed him and my purse and raced outside. My hand was shaking so much I had trouble getting the key in the ignition, but I locked all the doors, backed out of the driveway and kept backing halfway up the block. I didn't come closer until the police car arrived."

"That was smart. You couldn't be sure there wasn't somebody still in the house."

Her steadiness must have been a facade, because her fingers twisted together and he saw fear on her face. "Do you think he was?" she asked.

"He?" Seth repeated.

"I just assumed it would have to be a man… I mean, could a woman have enough strength to bludgeon someone to death like that?"

Not likely for a woman, but he wouldn't rule one out. "I doubt the killer was still in the house when you arrived home." Seth's guess that the murder had happened within the last half hour or so suggested the killer hadn't been gone long, though.

He asked her what cars she noticed parked on the street. She turned her head, telling him she recognized the pickup truck near the corner as belonging to the man who lived in that house. Otherwise…

"That almost has to be her car, doesn't it?" He followed her gaze to the sedan right in front of her car.

"I'll find out," he said, and continued to ask questions.

No, Ms. Boyd hadn't seen anyone outside or even looking through their windows when she turned onto the block and then into her own driveway, although she really hadn't paid attention. "Less than usual," she admitted. "Because my feet hurt."

"New shoes?"

"Yes, and I'm going to throw them away."

He smiled faintly, then asked, "Does anybody else have a key to your house?"

The way her hands continued to writhe, he was surprised he hadn't heard the snap of her knuckles cracking.

"The landlord must." She frowned. "And… I suppose Andrea might have had one. I guess she must have, or she couldn't have gotten in, could she?"

He didn't even try to hide the spike of anger. "You know the victim?"

Her gaze slid away from his.

"Any reason why she might have been in the house?"

"But there isn't any reason for her to be here. I mean, the real estate firm she works for also manages the property, but I haven't needed any repairs, and I can't imagine anyone complained that I was doing damage to the house. Why else would she have let herself in?" Alternating between determined poise and vulnerability, Ms. Boyd was now all but vibrating with indignation that spilled over. "I can't believe she's allowed to just do that. If I'd thought anyone could just poke through our stuff, I wouldn't have rented a house through that firm."

"I'll be talking to her boss, but I seriously doubt she was supposed to let herself into rentals when the tenants weren't there. That makes me wonder why she did. Have you heard from her in the recent past?"

Ms. Boyd shook her head. "Not a word. She showed me the house, I filled out the application, went into the real estate office to sign some paperwork and pay first and last months' rent. They gave me the key and that was it."

She and her son had lived here for eleven months, she said. And yes, she'd run into Andrea a few times since at the grocery store or pharmacy, so she must live here in town. They'd been friendly, in a casual way. "She'd ask how the house was working out, we might talk about some event here in town or the weather. Nothing really personal. I think she was only being polite."

"Is she married? Does she have children?"

Her forehead creased. "She's married, I'm

pretty sure, but I don't know about kids. I don't remember her saying anything."

His phone rang just then. He was relieved by the interruption, as he was undecided about how much more he wanted to ask her right now versus later. Particularly whether he should, bluntly or subtly, mention the physical resemblance between the two women.

After the brief conversation, he turned to her and said, "You won't be able to get back in your house for at least twenty-four hours, probably longer. Do you have a friend you can stay with?"

"But… I need some of Jacob's things. And mine!"

Her feet hurt, he remembered. "Give me a list of the most important things, and I'll see what I can do."

THE DETECTIVE'S EXPRESSION was completely uncompromising. He wasn't going to let them back in the house at all. The idea of going back in made Helen feel sick, anyway. She couldn't until the body was gone, and even then…how would she feel cooking in that kitchen? Walking right across the vinyl where Andrea had died, even when the blood had been washed away?

Not letting herself look at the man who

seemed to take up more space than he should, she pressed a hand to her stomach. "I don't know if I can keep living there."

He had unnervingly blue eyes, which she knew were intent on her face right now. Somehow, that intensity compelled her to turn her head and meet those eyes.

"Death doesn't have to contaminate a home," he said calmly.

"But murder?" Helen asked around the lump in her throat.

"You knew Andrea Sloan. Would she want to haunt you?"

All she felt was revulsion. "I don't know. How can I tell, when I have no idea why she was in my house?"

Detective Renner kept studying her for long enough to make her want to squirm. He must be a whiz at interrogations. Finally, he inclined his head. "Give yourself time. Tonight, it's probably best if you stay at a hotel."

Since he had that notebook handy, anyway, she dictated a list of essentials to him. "I can go buy some of the stuff if I have to, but I really need the blue stuffed bunny on Jacob's bed, and his blankie. It's probably on the sofa."

"Yellow?"

"Yes, that's it. The clothes and diapers and whatnot aren't as important. Oh, it would be good if you could grab his potty seat from the bathroom."

"Okay. I doubt it's a significant part of the crime scene." He smiled, got out and walked up to her rental, disappearing inside.

She rubbed her breastbone, as if to ease a strange pressure beneath it. Detective Renner had a nice smile, one that encouraged her to trust him, that crinkled the skin beside his eyes and softened the hard lines of an angular face she'd first thought looked dangerous. He wasn't handsome, exactly, not like Richard. God knew she'd never trust a smooth, well-dressed, handsome man again. But trusting this detective wasn't an option, either, even if he was a decent man.

Helen Boyd couldn't trust anyone, a cop least of all.

In fact, the smart thing for her to do was bolt, before this cop had a chance to look into her background and discover she didn't have one.

Her mind worked furiously, forming arguments on both sides. Running without changing identities wouldn't do any good. Unless she reverted to her previous one temporarily…? But what if Richard was watching for Megan Cobb? At least here in Lookout, she couldn't imagine that he'd make a move while the police were actively investigating a murder and keeping an eye on her, too.

Conclusion: she and Jacob were safest here for the moment.

She sagged, with no one to see her. She didn't have a lot of stuff, but hated the idea of taking off with only what they were wearing. They'd done that last time, and it had been hard to start completely over. This time around, she *couldn't* go without Jacob's blankie and his bunny.

She did keep a couple of packed bags ready, in case they had to bolt. She'd put family photos and other mementos in them, so she didn't have to carry them around in her purse all the time. Cash, too, and the birth certificate and driver's license that would turn her back into Megan Cobb. Plus changes of clothes for both of them.

Tomorrow, she'd decide what to do. Andrea Sloan's murder might not have anything to do with her.

And to think, she didn't usually allow herself any illusions.

At last, she pulled herself together enough to get out of the car again and go up to her neighbor's door. If only a chocolate chip cookie and milk could make her feel better. If it turned out Andrea had been killed in her place, Helen didn't know how she could go on. Except, of course, she had to. Jacob needed her.

Allie needed her, too, but she couldn't think about that, or crushing guilt might leave her unable to protect Jacob—and he had to come first.

Chapter Two

Seth was the sole detective on a police force that had only twelve sworn officers altogether, including the chief. If absolutely necessary, he could borrow an officer or two to help in an investigation. So far, beyond keeping the responding officer on the doorstep until the CSI team and morgue van arrived, Seth didn't want help. He preferred to talk to neighbors and then the husband himself.

He put off speaking to Ms. Boyd's boss until morning, but did call the day-care operator, who confirmed that Jacob's mother had picked him up about five minutes before the six o'clock deadline. Until the ME gave him a more informed time of death than he had so far, Seth couldn't rule out Ms. Boyd. She'd have had to go home to meet the victim, kill her and then pick up her little boy while appearing completely unperturbed. Hard to see her as that cold-blooded...but it was conceivable. It meant she was a hell of an actor, though. He really believed the seesawing emotions he'd seen were genuine.

That said, his instincts were sending up some flares. He suspected that Helen Boyd had secrets.

For now, he wanted to keep her cooperative, so after making his phone calls, he located a suitcase in the hall closet and filled it with the kid's clothes and toys first, including a blue stuffed rabbit, before invading her bedroom. He tossed sneakers into the suitcase first, took a pair of jeans off a pile in a bottom drawer, a T-shirt and zip-up sweatshirt from the middle drawer, then made himself open the top drawer. It was astonishingly neat, by his standards. He took out an oversize Eeyore T-shirt he presumed she wore as a nightgown, a plain beige cotton bra and two pairs of panties, then closed the drawer before thinking, *Wait.* Socks. He tossed two pairs in the suitcase, then went to the bathroom.

The crime scene investigators might not be happy with him, but he couldn't see what they'd learn from Ms. Boyd's clean clothes or her or her son's toothbrushes. He did peek in the medicine cabinet, which could often be revealing. In this case…nope. No prescription drugs. Only ibuprofen for her, cherry-flavored painkillers for Jacob, bath powder, floss and hair spray and gel. Stick deodorant, which he tossed into the suitcase along with the tooth-brushes and toothpaste.

A minute later, he carried the suitcase and plastic potty seat out to her living room, where he paused to pick up the thin, tattered blanket before going out to her now-empty car. He was taking advantage of unlocked doors to set everything on the back seat next to the boy's car seat when Ms. Boyd came hurrying out of the neighbor's house carrying her son.

She told him she'd go to the Lookout Inn, a pricey place to stay, but without driving a distance she didn't have a lot of choice. The bed-and-breakfast inns in town probably weren't any cheaper, and wouldn't afford as much privacy.

"All right," he said. "One more thing. Would you allow me to look in the trunk of your car without a warrant?"

She recoiled. "You think I— Of course you can look." Cheeks flushed, she handed over her car keys, then stayed where she was.

The trunk was as tidy as the floorboards of her car and the house. He did lift the cover to be sure no bloody pipe lurked beneath with the spare tire and jack. Nope.

After slamming the trunk lid, he gave her back the keys. "I may check on you later."

She looked less than happy at the idea, but dipped her head in apparent resignation and leaned into the car to fasten her drowsy son into his seat. A minute later, she drove off.

Left standing on the sidewalk, Seth watched the car proceed cautiously down the street until it turned out of sight. He swore under his breath and rolled his shoulders.

She left him unsettled. And he didn't think it was just the uncomfortable fact that she was an attractive woman.

After some thought, he decided part of the problem was that her responses had veered from the norm. Which led him back to where he'd started: Helen Boyd wasn't telling him all she was thinking, by a long shot. But what was she hiding?

HELEN JUMPED SIX inches at the soft knock on the door of the hotel room even though she'd expected it. She had horribly mixed feelings about seeing Detective Renner again tonight. She wanted to know what he'd learned, of course. How could she make decisions otherwise? But he made her nervous; he watched her with those penetrating blue eyes until she felt as if he was reading her mind.

He also wasn't the only one who could find her here. She approached the door cautiously. "Who is it?"

The detective's voice both reassured her and didn't. Like she had a choice about whether to let him in.

He dominated the room from the moment he stepped into it. She couldn't quite figure it out, since she had the feeling he was trying to be unassuming. Some of it was size; he certainly topped six feet, which made him a whole lot taller than she was. Broader, too, with impressive shoulders and a rangy, athletic build.

As she backed away, she decided unhappily that the quality was innate. The strength of his control and purpose, his determination, were impossible to miss. She wondered if his police chief or whoever was his direct boss ever dared to give him an order.

Of course, he started by assessing her with those sharp eyes before sweeping the room in search of…who knew? Enemies crouching behind the bed or peering from the closet? At last, his gaze settled on Jacob, sound asleep on one side of the queen-size bed. He looked so small in the big bed, so defenseless.

In a low voice, the detective asked, "Will we wake him if we talk?"

Helen shook her head, knowing her voice softened because of his concern. "An earthquake wouldn't wake him once he's really conked out. He's a very early riser, though."

His laugh was quiet and a little gravelly. It sent a shiver of reaction over her skin. "I won't keep you long." He still eyed Jacob as she led him to the pair of small upholstered club chairs by the window. "He's past needing a crib?"

"Oh, yes. He was only fifteen months old the first time he climbed out of his crib." She grimaced at the memory. "He fell, of course, screamed bloody murder—" She pressed her hands to her cheeks, feeling the heat. "That was a poor choice of words."

Another rumble of a laugh settled her nervousness a bit.

"Fortunately, he wasn't hurt, but we transitioned to a mattress on the floor pretty quick. Which turned me into the world's lightest sleeper. Every night, I imagine him wandering around the house while I sleep, completely unaware." Why was she babbling? "I may not get a good night's sleep again until he leaves home for college."

His smile was a little crooked. "According to my mother, that's no guarantee."

Helen gave a choked laugh. "Thank you for

that thought." She looked down at the table, clasped her hands together on her lap and struggled for calm before she lifted her chin again. "Have you found out anything?"

"Nothing to explain her death yet, I'm sorry to say. I was able to talk to her husband. You were right. The car at the curb was hers."

"What about children?" That possibility bothered her terribly.

"Two stepkids," he said. "Thirteen and fifteen. Her husband is ten years older than Ms. Sloan. The kids weren't home, so I can't say how they'll take her death."

With a huge lump in her throat, Helen only managed a nod.

"None of the neighbors saw anything helpful, unfortunately. Most weren't home until five thirty or later. Your Iris naps late every afternoon."

She closed her eyes momentarily. "I knew that."

He was silent until she looked at him again, when he said, "So now I have a problem." All traces of humor or sympathy had vanished from his face. The shadow of his evening stubble only made him appear more threatening. "I have to understand the connection between you and Ms. Sloan. It wasn't chance she was killed in your kitchen."

"I don't know!" Helen cried. "I don't *have* a relationship with the woman."

"After seeing the two of you, I might have guessed you were sisters," he said slowly.

"That's ridiculous," she protested, stiffening when she realized that hadn't come out as forcefully as she'd hoped. "Even in a town this size, there must be a lot of women with dark hair and brown eyes. And…and about the same height."

"Close enough in age to be twins." He sounded both thoughtful and inexorable. "And it's more than coloring. You have similar bone structure, noses. Straight on, I wouldn't mistake you for her, but at a quick glance…" Renner shrugged.

Light-headed, Helen could feel the speed of her pulse in her throat. Dear Lord, she should have run. Before this man got too curious about her.

"I don't understand." Her voice came out little more than a croak, but that was surely natural, given what he'd just suggested. "I'm a single mother. New in town. I haven't been on a date since my divorce. The only man at work who ever asked me out just got engaged to someone else. I do my job, and the rest of the time Jacob is my whole life. How could I have an enemy?"

"Ex-boyfriend. Ex-husband." Seemingly relaxed, he never looked away.

She could tell him. She could say, *I think my ex-husband murdered Andrea, thinking she was me*. But then what? Richard was sure to have an indisputable alibi—he'd have been in a meeting with someone like the Seattle city mayor or a congressman. Anyway, admitting to that much would mean revealing her real name—and Detective Renner would soon find a warrant for her arrest. If she'd killed a man in Seattle, why not a woman here in Lookout? Richard was smart enough not to have left so much as a fingerprint behind, she thought bitterly.

Fingerprints. Oh, dear God, if this detective submitted hers, a match would pop up immediately.

Panic pushed her to her feet. She grabbed the chair back for support. Voice shaking, she said, "I don't appreciate you scaring me this way. Maybe Andrea has been stealing from renters in every house she has keys to. She could have a partner that…that she betrayed somehow. Or a lover. What if they met in other people's homes during the day? Do you know *anything* about this woman?" She put everything she had into this scathing speech. "Or did you decide right away that I must be some kind of… I don't know, ex-CIA agent on the run, or a femme fatale with cast-off lovers hunting for me?"

Standing stiffly, she defied the detective's continued contemplation.

Seemingly unmoved by her defiance, he said, "I really hadn't gotten that far in my thinking. And of course my first assumption is that Ms. Sloan was the intended victim, not you. My hope was to get you thinking, in case there's something you're not telling me."

She pretended that wasn't a question. "This has been an upsetting day. I'd like you to go now."

His eyebrows flickered, but he bent his head in acknowledgment and rose to his feet as casually as if he'd made the decision himself. As he strolled to the door, he said, "I assumed you were already asking yourself these same questions, Ms. Boyd. You're smart enough to have been scared. It wasn't my intention to make it worse."

Helen didn't hold back a snort.

Almost to the door, Renner turned, expression inquiring.

"Of course you meant to scare me! Congratulations, you did a great job." At least that wasn't a lie.

"You're wrong," he said quietly. "Lock the

door behind me." He wasn't all the way out into the hall when he added in a much harder voice, "I'll expect you not to leave the area. Do you understand?"

"Yes!" She felt herself vibrating with tension. No chance he wouldn't be able to see that.

"As long as you're not her killer, I'm on your side, you know." He nodded and closed the door behind him.

Helen leaped forward and, with shaking hands, turned the dead bolt and hooked on the probably useless chain. Then she stood still and strained to hear any sound from the hall, with no idea whether he still stood there or was walking away.

In listening to that silence, she had a horrifying thought. If Richard had killed Andrea, where was he now? Had he been somewhere he could watch when she arrived home and the police responded? If he had, he'd know where she was—and he'd have seen Jacob. And that was assuming the private investigator who'd trailed her in Southern California hadn't seen Jacob.

A dry sob escaped her. Who was she kidding? To know she had a child, Richard had only had to step inside her house. The high chair at the table alone would tell him.

Most of her desperation to escape him had been to ensure he never knew she was pregnant. There was no possibility that he was capable of being any kind of parent. He was the kind of man who lashed out without warning, both verbally and physically. He could smile, wish their dinner guests good-night, close the door and knock her to the floor because she'd done or said something earlier that had displeased him. Even with his housekeeper and a nanny as a buffer, an active boy would try his nonexistent patience. He'd search for her qualities in Jacob and determine to eradicate them, along with Jacob's every memory of her.

This kind of terror was like being shaken by a vicious earthquake. Even though she'd been sure he had found them once before, she'd let herself get complacent since she moved to Lookout. She liked her job, and Jacob was a happy boy. Their little house had felt safe.

They would *never* be safe. She couldn't forget again. He wouldn't give up; she knew that. Monsters didn't. The best she could do was stay a step ahead. Which meant leaving, as soon as she could figure out how.

Oh, dear God. What if Richard, too, was staying at the Lookout Inn.

With a muffled cry, she darted across the room to test the lock on the slider that led out onto a balcony.

SETH LAY AWAKE for long stretches that night. Every time he dozed off, he'd find himself starting awake, adrenaline firing through his body like an electrical shock.

Gritting his teeth and punching his pillow into a new shape, he had to convince himself repeatedly that there wasn't anything else he could have done before morning.

Except, maybe, sleep in the hall outside Helen Boyd's room at the inn to make sure she didn't disappear—and that a killer didn't get to her and that cute kid of hers.

He groaned and rested his forearm over his eyes. Damn it, the woman was right; his initial focus *should* be on the actual victim's life, her character, her husband, friends and acquaintances. And it was—he'd talked to her husband for the first time this evening, but he'd go back as many times as he had to. Tomorrow, he'd talk to her boss and coworkers, get the names of friends. Find out if there was even a whisper suggesting she had a lover or might be up to something illicit.

But he'd always paid attention to his gut, and while Helen was trying hard to play the outraged innocent, she wasn't a good liar. And she *was* lying; he had no doubt about that. All he had to do was look at the turmoil in her eyes that should be transparent instead of clouded with a darkness he didn't think was entirely caused by her discovery today of a dead body in her house.

He couldn't see her as a killer, but he had to be damn sure he was thinking like a cop, not a man drawn to a woman. He couldn't afford to let himself have even a momentary thought about her as an attractive woman.

Damn. Seth sat up in bed and swung his feet to the floor. He remained there for a minute, head hanging. If he fell asleep with that picture in his head, he risked having an erotic dream involving a woman he would almost certainly interview again in a murder investigation. A woman who'd looked like she hated him by the time she insisted he leave her hotel room.

Not happening.

Even though he wasn't hungry, he scrambled eggs and ate breakfast to fill the last dark hour before dawn. Then he showered and drove to Hood River to attend the autopsy.

The medical examiner didn't come up

with any surprises. Andrea Sloan was in good health generally. She had been killed by a blow to the head. The ME thought the weapon used was a short length of pipe, considerably fatter than the tire iron in the trunk of Ms. Boyd's car. The victim had also taken a blow to her side that had broken ribs, probably postmortem. A kick, the ME suggested.

Seth would walk through the house again today now that he had a warrant, but felt sure he wouldn't find the weapon. The garage was his best possibility, but he'd looked in the window and guessed Ms. Boyd, at least, went in there only to retrieve the lawn mower and return it when she was finished cutting the grass.

He was at the real estate office when it opened, where he started with the victim's coworkers, all horrified by the news of Andrea's death. He was assured that she was likable, charming, energetic, with the best sales record in the office. He also learned that she didn't work on the property management side of the business.

The owner of the office, a woman in her fifties, explained that Andrea had sold a couple of properties for a man named Dean Ziegler, as well as a house to him, and as a favor had agreed to manage his rentals. At Seth's request, Tina Daley dug in the records, reporting that Ziegler owned an apartment house with ten units and three rental homes.

The only key to any of those units missing was the one Seth had collected as evidence.

Andrea's assistant, a young woman in her twenties named Brooke Perry, insisted she'd have known if Andrea had received a phone call about a problem at one of the rental homes.

"The only reason I can imagine she'd have been there was if the renter had asked to see her." Her forehead creased. "Or if Mr. Ziegler wanted to meet her, or insisted she inspect the house, I suppose. But I really think she'd have said if he'd called." She hesitated. "I was surprised when she left at five thirty. That was early for her."

"Did she say anything about where she was going?"

Brooke bit her lip. "She said something like, 'I don't have any appointments, and anything else can wait for tomorrow.'"

A tomorrow that would never come for her.

Seth asked for Ziegler's number and address. The man was evidently retired as a vice president with a local bank. Seth called, found he was home and drove to a spectacular Tuscan-style mansion on a bluff above the river.

Turning, he saw Mount Hood seemingly hovering almost near enough to touch, too. Hell of a view all around.

Ziegler turned out to be a slim, silver-haired man who was well-preserved for the seventy-three years old the DMV records said he was.

"I'm shocked," he repeated several times. "Why would anyone want to hurt Andrea? She's good at her job because people like her."

Once they were seated in an enormous living room with gleaming wood floors and a wall of windows looking out at the river, he spread his hands and said, "Tell me how I can help you."

Seth couldn't decide how genuine that was, but explained that, at this point, he was trying to get to know the victim, in a manner of speaking. "Hobbies, friends, any problems in her life, of course."

"Problems? I really don't think she had any. Well, maybe two." Ziegler smiled wryly. "Both teenagers."

"The stepkids."

"Defiant fifteen-year-old boy, sulky thirteen-year-old girl." He shrugged. "My sense is that she actually had an okay relationship with them. She'd laugh telling me about them. They're just at difficult ages."

Fifteen-year-old boys had been known to

kill before…but to follow a stepmother to a house where she wasn't supposed to be, then take her down with a single, powerful blow? Seth didn't believe it.

"I've met her husband a few times," Ziegler continued. "Nice guy. Did you know he's in banking, too? Manages a branch here in town."

Seth did know that. It had crossed his mind that a real estate agent and a banker could be up to something questionable together, but again…why was Andrea at the rental? In fact, trespassing in it?

"Andrea did have a certain reserve," Ziegler commented. "I sometimes thought she had to work at being as outgoing as she appeared to her clients." He frowned. "I do believe her warmth was genuine, and she and Russ had a connection those of us who've been divorced three times can only envy."

Seth left a card and asked the guy to call if he thought of anything that might be helpful in uncovering the reason she'd been targeted.

If she was, he thought again, as he drove down the winding, paved lane from the house.

Next on Seth's agenda was to stop at the craft brewery where Andrea Sloan's husband, Russell, had supposedly met two friends right after the bank closed at five o'clock. According to him, he'd left his car in the bank parking lot and walked to the brewery. Andrea had let him know not to expect her before six thirty or seven.

When Seth asked if she had said why she'd be late, he'd answered dully, "She didn't work conventional hours. Weekends, evenings…" He shrugged. "When somebody looking to buy is free, she made herself available. We didn't eat dinner most nights until seven thirty or eight."

There wasn't any chance Ziegler had intended to sell Helen's rental, was there? Seth asked himself belatedly. That nobody had told her yet?

Sitting outside the brewery, situated in a handsome old brick building in the oldest part of town, Seth called the man and asked.

"No, as long as I can keep a tenant in it, a little house like that makes more money for me than I'd get from selling it."

"She hadn't recommended you sell?"

"She never said a word about it, and I didn't, either."

Seth went into the brewery and asked to speak to the manager. A man with a billiard-ball bare and shiny head came out. Prematurely balding, Seth guessed, since the guy didn't appear much older than he was.

"Sure, I know Russ Sloan," he said readily. "He's one of a group of other professionals and downtown merchants who gather here often. He was in yesterday afternoon, in fact."

At Seth's request, he reran security footage that showed Sloan walking in with a second man at 5:11, both laughing, and leaving just before 6:30. Unless he'd hired a killer, that let him off the hook. Especially since finding a hit man wasn't as easy as many people thought.

Seth thanked him and went back out to his car.

It would take a big slice of his day, but he wanted to talk to Ms. Boyd's boss in person. He could grab some lunch on the way.

Chapter Three

Two days had passed since Andrea was murdered, and Helen sat on the edge of the bed watching Jacob fitting pieces into one of his simple puzzles. He'd been really good, considering his routine had been turned on end. *She* was the one on the verge of a breakdown. All her mind did was spin with thoughts and fears interspersed with pictures, starting with that single high-heeled shoe lying on her kitchen floor and ending up with Detective Renner's narrowed eyes as he asked questions that told her he thought *she* might have killed Andrea.

Mixed in were fleeting memories of the moment she realized she was pregnant. The surge of love when her newborn son was placed in her arms.

To top it all off, both mornings when she'd gotten dressed, she was reminded that Detective Renner had handled all these clothes, including her underwear. Did he notice the practicality of everything she wore? Helen hated that thought.

Having the phone ring was a welcome novelty.

But who else? It was Detective Renner, letting her know she could return to her rental house. "I've taken the tape down," he said tersely.

She wanted to ask about the blood but didn't. She could clean it up. She could. Living there with the constant awareness a woman had been killed in the kitchen, a woman who had likely died in her place…that was something else altogether.

The weight of guilt clashed with the ever-burning determination to keep Jacob away from Richard. If he'd found her there instead of Andrea…he'd have Jacob right now. Her family might not even know for ages, and unless he was convicted of murder, they'd lose if they took her ex-husband to court to contest custody. Her whole reason for being was to keep her son safe, give him a chance to grow up knowing he was loved.

"Thank you for letting me know," she said politely.

"I'd suggest having the locks changed and consider installing a security system."

No matter what she did, she wouldn't feel

safe in that house, but the reality was that she couldn't afford to keep staying at a hotel. Conserving her money was especially important now.

"Your landlord might agree to bear the cost," the detective continued. "Especially since it was his employee killed in your place."

That gave her a tiny lift of hope. He was right. But no matter what, she'd pay to have the locks changed. Now, today, even if that cost extra.

A security system would be reassuring if she intended to stay any length of time…but she didn't. Of course, she couldn't tell the detective she planned to disappear as soon as she could.

"Yes, all right," she said, realizing Renner was probably waiting for a response. "Do you know any more?"

"I haven't made an arrest, if that's what you're asking." He spoke curtly, betraying frustration. "Which means I'd like to sit down with you again, Ms. Boyd."

Her throat constricted. Could she hold him off long enough to make preparations for starting over again?

Did she have a choice?

"I suppose you'll find me there. If I pack

up and check out right away, I won't have to pay for another night here."

"Then I'll meet you at the house."

Just to make her day better.

Setting down the phone, she bent to kiss Jacob. "We're going home, kiddo. You finish putting your puzzle together while I pack."

He lifted his head. "Hot dog?"

"You're hungry?"

He nodded vigorously. Hot dogs were his current favorite food, although mac and cheese was right up there, too. While staying here, they'd eaten makeshift breakfasts in the room, gone out to lunch each day and used room service for dinner. Darkness felt too dangerous; they were safer staying behind locked doors.

Fortunately, she was pretty sure there were hot dogs in the freezer at home. "We'll have lunch. *Maybe* a hot dog."

It didn't take her ten minutes to throw everything into the suitcase. Jacob was fascinated by the lobby attendant who insisted on taking both the suitcase and potty seat out to her car.

In the past year, he'd gone through a stage of being painfully shy with everyone for no discernible reason, just recently becoming more curious and ready to grin at complete strangers. Maybe earlier she'd infected him with her tension, and as she felt safer his confidence returned. Kids undoubtedly reacted to their parents' subtlest cues.

She locked the car even before she started it, as she always did. As she drove out of the lot, she craned her neck trying to see if anyone was paying attention to them. Disconcerted, she saw that Jacob, too, was turning to look around.

With this being a working day, there wasn't much activity. From what she'd been told, tourist season didn't really boom for another week or two, once schools let out. You wouldn't know that looking at the windsurfing business next door, though. She knew vaguely that they rented small boats as well as windsurfing equipment. Like much of the rest of June, today was sunny but still chilly, and she could see multicolored sails swelling with the wind out on the choppy water. If someone over there was keeping an eye out for her, she'd never be able to pick him out.

She was quite sure nobody followed her home—but then, Richard or anyone he hired wouldn't have to follow her to know where she was going. Leaving their stuff in the car, she carried Jacob inside, setting him down on the sofa with his blue bunny.

"Wait right there for me," she said sternly.

He bounced on his butt. "Hurry, Mommy."

Battling extreme reluctance, she steeled herself to look in the kitchen. She couldn't let Jacob see the blood…

But the vinyl floor was spotless. No dead body, no blood.

Well, she'd known the body would be taken away, but she didn't think police officers would clean up crime scenes.

Helen stared. Squeezed her eyes shut and opened them again. Still clean. She'd scrub the floor herself once Jacob was napping, just to be sure, but somebody had done this for her.

Thinking of the man who managed to be both unrelenting and occasionally thoughtful, she had a good idea who'd done it. The kindness weakened her, even if he'd been thinking about Jacob and not her at all.

"I want hot dog," her son reminded her.

Helen laughed. "Okay, okay!"

She raced through the house, looking in closets and pushing the shower curtain aside before dashing out to get their bags. She didn't see a soul. Everyone must be at work, and even Iris's car was missing.

Fortunately, Helen found buns in the freezer as well as an unopened package of hot dogs. If she heated a can of baked beans and peeled some carrots, the meal would be perfectly adequate.

Jacob hadn't gotten through half of his hot dog and one carrot stick when the doorbell rang. He started wriggling like an eel to slither out of his high chair.

"No way," she told him, but had to lift him out to go to the front door. Escape artist that he was, she couldn't leave him alone for a second when he was high enough to take a fall. He'd figure out how to unsnap the belt anytime now, she felt sure.

Hand on the dead bolt, she raised her voice. "Who is it?"

"Detective Renner."

With the usual mixed feelings he inspired, she unlocked and opened the door. Jacob bounced in her arms. As soon as he saw the detective, he grinned and exclaimed, "Boo!"

Renner laughed. "Boo to you, too."

Just as well that no two-year-old could grasp the concept of a police officer, or wonder why he kept wanting to talk to mommy.

"We're finishing lunch," she said.

"No problem."

When they got to the kitchen and she lifted Jacob to put him in his high chair, he struggled.

"No!"

The debate was short. He was done with lunch, or just refused to be confined again, she wasn't sure. She had to find one of those plastic seats that would boost him to table height. He'd be a lot happier. It amazed her that her thoughts could seamlessly shift to ordinary mommy mode under the circumstances.

Helen didn't let Jacob watch much TV but decided to make an exception. He climbed up onto the sofa, grabbing his blankie, while she pulled up a video.

She turned to see that Renner waited in the doorway to the kitchen, watching. Of course he was; she might be hiding a cache of diamonds in the cushions of the couch along with all the crumbs.

Her shoulder brushed his arm when she hurried into the kitchen. Finding she'd lost her own appetite, she cleared the table, then decided grudgingly that she ought to at least offer him a cup of coffee.

"Instant," she warned.

"That's fine." His mouth quirked. "I'm not picky."

Dumping a spoonful of grounds in her own mug, she said, "A cappuccino would taste really good right now. Unfortunately, having one regularly is not in my budget."

"You can dump a lot of money really fast

at those coffee drive-throughs," he agreed. "Although—" He stopped so fast, she almost heard the brakes screeching.

"Although what?" She eyed him suspiciously.

He gave his head a shake. "I was going to say something completely inappropriate. Can we forget about it?"

Inappropriate? What could he have been thinking? Her cheeks felt warm, but she needed to know. Still hovering at the stove, she asked, "If I absolve you in advance, will you tell me?"

"You can afford the calories. That's what I was thinking."

Oh, good, nice to know he thought she was too skinny. Stress had a way of doing that to her, and she lived with a steady dose. Even pregnant, she'd had trouble gaining enough weight.

He wouldn't have been thinking any such thing unless he'd noticed her body in a way that had nothing to do with any crime committed. The recognition he might be attracted to her was only momentary. Yes, he was undeniably sexy. But if all went well, she wouldn't see him again, because she and Jacob would be as far away as she could manage, as soon as possible.

Emotions flat again, she poured water into the mugs and carried them to the table. Renner declined her offer of milk and sugar, both of which she dumped generously in her mug.

"I should be fat," she said lightly. "Hot dogs, cheeseburgers, macaroni and cheese. We don't eat the way I did before I had Jacob."

The detective laughed. "I'm sure." He was nice enough not to mention that the foods she'd named also happened to be cheap, not just appealing to a toddler's taste buds.

Helen stirred her coffee. Procrastination had its appeal, but she wasn't a fan. "I don't understand what it is you think I can tell you," she said.

His expression changed. More accurately, vanished. He had a flat, guarded look that might be normal for a cop on the job.

"When is the last time you saw Andrea Sloan?"

She shook her head. "You're looking for some connection that doesn't exist. But let me think…" Grocery store? No, there'd been once since then. "I was jogging. Mostly, I take Jacob in his stroller, but that day Iris kept him. Andrea runs, too. I'd forgotten that. We came face-to-face, jogged in place for a minute to exchange pleasantries, then went our separate ways. It was… I don't know, six weeks ago? Two months?"

"Did you know she jogged?"

Helen shook her head. "Not until then."

"Were you dressed alike?"

She didn't like the way he'd fixated on their resemblance. "No, she wore a brand name, formfitting running set and, I'm sure, top-of-the-line running shoes. Me, I wear a T-shirt and sweats or shorts depending on the season and weather." She remembered inwardly cringing that day at what Andrea probably thought of her outfit.

"Pleasantries?" he asked.

"Chilly, but at least it's not raining. House is still working out great. Nice to see you."

A smile showed in his eyes, she'd swear it did.

"No calls since then?"

"No."

"Can you think of any reason at all she would have wanted to speak to you?"

"No! It doesn't make sense. If this weren't such a small town, I'd have probably never run into her again after I signed the rental agreement. You can see yourself that I haven't trashed the place—"

As if she'd crashed into a plate-glass window, a horrifying thought struck her. What if

Richard had called or stopped by the real estate office, asking questions about her? Could Andrea have come by to warn her? If Richard or his hired hand had made her nervous enough, she might have let herself into the house to be less visible.

Yes, but if he'd actually seen Andrea, how could he have made the mistake?

But he might not have, Helen reminded herself. Andrea's assistant might have told her that a man was hunting for Helen, or Richard might have called rather than showing up in person.

Helen jumped up. "I have to check on Jacob." She found him asleep, thumb slipping out of his mouth.

With the remote, she turned off the movie and TV, then gently picked him up. She straightened, to see that, once again, Renner had followed. "Naptime," she murmured.

He nodded.

At least he didn't follow her. Jacob never opened his eyes as she laid him down and tucked him in, then pulled his door almost closed.

Renner didn't return to his seat at the kitchen table until she did.

"You thought of something, didn't you?"

Her heart picked up tempo. "Something?"

"About Ms. Sloan."

"I don't know what you're talking about," she said flatly.

He studied her speculatively. "Oh, I think you do."

"I had nothing to do with a woman I hardly know getting murdered in my kitchen." That sounded almost panicky. What did it matter? But she had to get rid of him. "I don't want to talk to you anymore without a lawyer."

WHATEVER SHE'D THOUGHT had scared the life out of her, and, man, Seth wanted to know what it was. Almost forty-eight hours had passed since Andrea Sloan had died, and he had no more idea why she'd been killed now than he had at the beginning. The one and only person he'd spoken to during this investigation who was acting squirrely was this woman. And he wanted to know why.

"I haven't accused you of anything," he said mildly. "I don't believe you killed Ms. Sloan." Which was true. But she knew something, he'd bet on it.

She crossed her arms, as if holding herself together. "Is your name Seth?"

"What?"

"I'm sorry—" Hot spots of color appeared on her cheekbones.

"Don't be sorry."

"It's not like I'd use—I mean, I'll still call you Detective—I just…" She shook her head, unable or unwilling to explain.

He could hope she would be less intimidated if she thought of him by his first name—except that he needed her running a little scared of him.

And, yeah, he hated that.

"Where did you live before you rented this place?" he asked abruptly.

Any color had drained from her face. "Los Angeles. North Hollywood, to be exact."

Truth, he thought. "Why did you move?"

"I wanted to raise Jacob someplace where we could get to know our neighbors, where he could safely ride a bike when he gets old enough. I spotted a listing for my current job online, researched the area and applied."

That sounded reasonable, although he wondered. "Does Jacob's father see him?"

Her back stiffened. "He didn't want children and has no interest in Jacob."

Now there, Seth thought, was a lie. "Where does he live?"

"LA."

"His name?"

"Richard—" Anger flared in her eyes. "It's none of your business. You can't contact him!"

Her alarm was very real, but Seth reminded himself that there could be a lot of reasons for her sensitivity with the subject that had absolutely nothing to do with the murder he was investigating. If she'd been an abused woman, for example, he didn't want to draw the abuser's attention to her, or the boy. On the other hand, what if she didn't have legal custody? That would explain some of what he was seeing, and it wasn't something he could ignore as an officer of the law. One thing he did know: Jacob was her son. Their resemblance was unmistakable.

Right now, he'd lose her if he kept pushing.

"You color your hair," he heard himself say.

She jerked back and lifted a hand to her head. "What makes you say that?" Her lips thinned as she realized she'd given herself away. "That *really* isn't any of your business."

No, it wasn't, but he'd been intrigued by her creamy skin from their first meeting. She had a redhead's complexion, freckles and a redheaded son.

"That was intrusive," he agreed. "I apologize. You have beautiful skin, and it made me think—" Damn, he was stepping in it here.

Helen Boyd studied him from those gold-flecked caramel eyes that were every bit as pretty as her skin. Then she sighed. "Yes, I color my hair. I always hated being a redhead."

"What about your eyebrows?" His mouth was running away from him.

"I...sometimes touch them up." She blushed, something she must do easily with that skin.

For a minute that stretched too long, they stared at each other. He drank in the rare sight of her sitting absolutely still, her lips parted as if she'd been on the verge of speaking. Her chin, he couldn't help noticing, was a little on the square, stubborn side.

She was the first to wrench her gaze away. "Are you done with your questions?"

"Yes." Seth had to clear his throat. "For now."

What had he been *thinking*? Coming on to a person of interest, if not a suspect, in an investigation was inexcusable. He had to get out of here, now, before he couldn't resist touching her.

Helen didn't even stand when he did, although when he reached the front door he realized she had followed, still keeping her distance. Seth opened the door and turned to face her.

"Let me repeat that I'm here to help, if you need it. You're worried about something. I wish you'd tell me what."

He might as well not have bothered to speak. She'd shuttered her expression and only waited. He'd go, but needed to be sure she'd taken seriously his concern about her security.

"Have you spoken to your landlord?"

"I left a message at the property management company, but I also called a locksmith. He's supposed to be here at four to change the locks."

"Good," Seth said softly. He nodded and left.

HELEN LOCKED THE door then slumped against it, feeling so much she couldn't identify.

Had any man ever looked at her like that?

Yes, the last time she was attracted to one. Richard.

His burning gaze had convinced her he wanted her desperately, loved her. She'd been such a fool, let herself be manipulated, controlled. Never again, she'd vowed. Not a vow she could afford to forget. So why was she getting weak in the knees because Seth Renner had implied he thought she was beautiful, had claimed she could depend on him?

Oh, the answer was simple enough. She had needs, but unlike women who allowed themselves to be deluded over and over again, Helen wouldn't dare succumb to temptation.

Her fierce need to protect Jacob would keep her from being that dumb. Even if she met a wonderful man who truly was everything he seemed to be, she'd have to lie to him, and what kind of relationship would that be? Lies corroded. Lies kept her from making friends, even.

For Jacob, she'd do anything.

While he napped, she'd make a plan instead of letting her thoughts run in panicked circles.

Helen went back to the kitchen, dumped out both mugs of barely touched coffee, and fetched a pen, notepad and her last bank statement. She had never done online banking. That took another kind of trust.

Would Seth… No, no, no. Would *Detective Renner* think to flag her bank account? Ask the bank, maybe, to inform him if she closed out the account, or withdrew a substantial amount of the balance? *Could* he do that legally?

Sure he could. All he'd have to do was get a warrant.

Well then, she'd assume he had. If she dared take at least a few days, even a week, she could stop by an ATM daily. She had to believe that Richard wouldn't be an immediate threat. Even he might have been shaken to discover he'd killed the wrong woman.

What if he thought he'd been *pursuing* the wrong woman? That Andrea lived in this house—she'd had a key, after all—that there'd been a mistake made and his ex-wife wasn't actually in the vicinity? Hope shimmered briefly as Helen wondered if Richard had gone back to Seattle to berate his private detective for being wrong?

The hope was shortlived. He would have checked the ID in Andrea's purse. The license plate on her car. Neither would match the name of the woman who rented this house, the one the private detective had identified as her.

Still, he'd back off, surely, until the investigation petered out and a cop wasn't coming by the house daily.

She hadn't checked him out online in at least a week, and obviously that had been a mistake. Helen opened her laptop and entered his name.

He popped up immediately in a *Seattle Times* article about a political event held yesterday evening. She kept searching, found mention of a dinner he was to host this coming Saturday to raise money for a congressional candidate launching a primary assault on an incumbent who had probably infuriated Richard by ignoring his advice.

Helen sat thinking. Saturday was two days away. Portland wasn't that long a drive from Seattle. Still, he'd want to be careful. When he first began hitting her, she'd thought he was losing his temper, that he lacked self-control but was genuinely shocked and sorry. Over months she came to understand that he was never careless in a way that might come back to reflect on *him*. No, his sense of self-preservation was finely tuned.

She'd have until Sunday or even Monday, she decided. She could mostly empty her bank account with three-to five-hundred-dollar withdrawals, followed by a bigger one on her way out of town. And, of course, she had the emergency cash she kept stashed in the to-go bags tucked behind some junk in the garage.

That would give her time this weekend to prowl a cemetery or two in Portland—or better yet, across the river in Vancouver, Washington. Surely, she could find the grave of a girl child who, if she'd lived, would be close to Helen's age. Once she and Jacob were a safe distance away, she'd request a birth certificate.

Tomorrow, she'd better go back to work. She needed to live as unremarkably as possible until she was ready to go.

Chapter Four

"Mommy! Don't go!" Tears pouring down his face, Jacob clung with all his strength to Helen's neck.

Close to crying herself, she continued to kneel just inside the front door of the day care, holding him. Jenna Fischer, the young woman who operated the home day care, crouched, too.

"Jacob," she coaxed, "Neil's been waiting for you to play trucks with him."

He wailed.

What else could she do but leave him? If she didn't go to work, she'd draw unwanted attention. Anyway, succumbing to his pleas would set a precedent that would come back to bite her. She'd never had to wrench his hands off her, but this morning might be a first.

"Jacob." She did her best to sound firm and hide how distraught she felt at his misery. "Honey." She gave him a small shake. "You like spending your day with Jenna and Neil and Evan. And even Courtney," she teased.

He shook his head hard. She thought his tears had slowed.

"Okay, maybe not Courtney. But she's not so bad, is she?"

Jacob didn't yet care whether his friends were girls or boys. But Courtney, almost four years old, was bossy. According to Jenna, most of the time the three boys did what Courtney ordered them to do, because she was good at organizing games. Helen could tell that Jacob, at least, felt a glimmer of resentment.

"We're having macaroni and cheese for lunch today," Jenna said, smiling. "*And* ice-cream sandwiches."

Sniffling, he wiped his wet cheeks on Helen's blouse. Oh, well. She was a mother. It was a rare day she made it to work unwrinkled and completely stain free.

At last, he reluctantly let Helen go and took Jenna's hand. Walking out, she suspected that he'd quickly forget he hadn't wanted her to go and start playing with his friends. If only it was so easy for her.

The last sight of his woeful expression and puffy, red eyes was sure to stick with her all day.

And that wasn't even the worst of it, she

thought tensely as she waited in a short line at the bank drive-up ATM. If Richard now knew about Jacob's existence, everything had changed. Was he safe at the home day care? Most of the time Jenna kept the doors locked, but toward the end of the day, the door was open for the pickups.

Would Jenna not want to keep Jacob if Helen talked to her about being extra careful because she was concerned about her ex-husband?

She withdrew three hundred dollars and pulled out of the bank parking lot, only to immediately get stuck at a red light. Her gaze flicked to the dashboard clock. She should have waited to do her errand after work.

As if the inside of her head was a pinball machine, her thoughts bounced back to Jacob. If she intended to stay in town, she could move him to a larger day care. Except he would always be vulnerable while she was at work.

Plus, if he didn't want to be left at Jenna's, imagine if she tried to drop him off mornings at a strange place full of adults and kids he didn't know! No, she couldn't do that to him. But, oh God, what if…?

Don't think about it.

By the time she reached her office, stowed her purse in a drawer and responded to an instant message from her boss, her facade of calm felt paper-thin.

BY MIDMORNING, SETH had completed background searches on Andrea's husband and several of her coworkers. He'd made good progress looking at her closest friends, too, as well as their husbands. Dean Ziegler; the fact that he and Andrea were both married to other people didn't mean they hadn't hooked up. Maybe she was trying to break it off and Ziegler didn't like that. Seth had to seriously consider him, given that he owned Helen's rental house and presumably had kept a key.

But so far, the only search that had raised red flags for Seth was the one he'd done on Helen Marie Boyd.

To all appearances, she'd emerged naked from the sea, as in Botticelli's painting, *The Birth of Venus*.

Damn it, he had to quit thinking about her that way.

Supposedly, she'd lived and worked last in California. If so, she had had still been using her married name. That was assuming Boyd was her maiden name. That would explain the giant blank where her history ought to be.

Seth just didn't believe in either possibility, in part because he had failed to find a divorce including that name in any Southern California county.

He also couldn't forget the turmoil he saw in her eyes. The darkness he guessed was fear. There could be a lot of reasons for that, especially after she found the dead woman in her kitchen. Even before he pointed out Andrea's resemblance to Helen, she'd thought about the possibility another woman had died in her place. He'd put money on it.

Why did he suspect she was as afraid of him because of the badge he wore as she was of whatever trouble followed her?

Irritated at himself, Seth shook his head. The fact that he was a cop might not have anything to do with her lack of trust. She didn't know him. It was equally possible that she'd been living in a gray area legally.

He brooded for a good ten minutes before deciding all he could do was show up on her doorstep over and over and over again, until she *did* know him.

HE RANG HER doorbell at six forty, figuring she and her boy would have eaten by now.

Her car was there in the driveway, but he didn't hear a sound until the door abruptly opened and she appeared, arms crossed, looking less than happy. "I told you I wouldn't talk to you again without my lawyer being present."

He lifted the bag he carried in his left hand. "I come bearing gifts this time."

She didn't so much as glance at the bag. "You've asked me a million questions already."

"I have," he agreed. "Fair warning—you won't get rid of me until I figure out who killed Andrea Sloan."

"Because you think I did it."

He frowned. She hadn't believed his previous reassurances. "No, I actually don't, but I do believe you're part of the answer."

Her eyes flickered, shadows falling where they hadn't been an instant before. After a moment, she opened the door wider and stepped back.

He hid his relief. She was well within her rights to insist on that lawyer, but was apparently relenting. It was also possible she couldn't afford to hire any attorney worth having, but had thought the threat would be enough.

"You shouldn't open the door without knowing who wants in," he said as he walked in.

"I peeked out the window."

"You might want to get a peephole installed. The better ones give you a good view of your porch while you're standing several feet back from the door."

Helen gave a wry look over her shoulder as she led him to the kitchen. "While I'm at it, why not have surround the house with barbed-wire fencing?"

Seth cleared his throat. "That might be a little extreme."

"Mommy?" Wearing denim overalls and a miniature, bright red cowboy hat, her son popped out of his room down the hall. Seeing Seth, he grinned and raced toward them, skidding to a stop at the last minute to grip his mom's leg.

"Jacob." Seth smiled down at him. "I like the hat."

The boy swept it off and held it out to Seth.

"I don't think it would fit me." Seth took it and settled it back on Jacob's head. Then he tipped up the brim with one finger. "There. Get along, partner."

"Giddyup!" The kid galloped down the hall, then back, giggling by the time he reached them.

"Have you eaten yet?" Seth asked.

Her brown eyes widened. "I'm afraid so. That's not what—" She nodded at the bag.

"No, but I'm hoping you haven't had *d-e-s-s-e-r-t*."

"You're trying to bribe me."

"You'd be doing me a favor to take this off my hands," he lied.

Helen rolled her eyes. "Let's see what you have."

"Actually," he said, taking the lidded plastic container out of the bag and setting it on the counter, "this is courtesy of my father. A couple of ladies in his neighborhood are constantly baking goodies for him. He grumbled that he had to let out his belt a notch just last week." Seth peeled off the lid. "Tiramisu cheesecake and oatmeal raisin cookies."

She peered in at the cheesecake, already sliced, and the dozen or so cookies. "I accept."

A minute later, Jacob sat in his high chair to eat his cookie and drink milk from his sippy cup. Helen poured coffee for herself and Seth, and served the cheesecake on plates.

She slipped a first bite into her mouth and made a humming sound, obviously savoring the sugary treat before she finally swallowed. "Have you *tasted* this?"

He shifted uncomfortably. "No," he said, a little hoarsely.

"If I were your father, I'd marry the woman who made this."

Seth gave a rough chuckle. "She drives Dad crazy. Anyway, as far as I can tell, he's not interested in remarrying."

"Really?" Her forehead furrowed. "Are your parents divorced?" Helen made a sound that was too sharp to be a laugh. "Wow. Listen to me, pretending you're not here to interrogate me. And eating your food." She pushed her plate away.

"Please." Without thinking, he covered her hand with his. "I didn't want to take all this home. I thought you and Jacob could enjoy it. Please," he repeated, looking from her face to his hand, still resting on hers. He felt quivering tension and the fineness of the bones beneath his fingertips and palm.

Damn.

He pulled his hand back. What kind of idiot was he? That she, too, slipped occasionally into thinking of him as a man rather than a detective didn't help, only heightening his awareness of her.

This moment, he absolutely could not tell what she was thinking. She did pull the plate back toward her and, after a tiny hesitation, resume eating.

Breaking the tension, Jacob demanded, and got, another cookie. Seth asked what he'd done today, then tried to piece the answer together from an indignant insistence that Neil had hit him, but Jenna told a story with puppets and they ate mac cheese and he didn't *want* to go to Jenna's today, he wanted to stay with Mommy. At least, that's what Seth thought he'd said. Some of his words were clear, some incomprehensible, although Seth could tell the boy's mother understood every one.

At last Helen lifted him to the floor. While she was still bent over, he whispered something.

She ran her hand gently over his head and smiled, her face softening. "Yes, you may play with your animals for a few minutes, but then it will be bedtime."

He scampered away, her gaze following him. The tenderness changed to worry.

"Usually, he loves his day care, but today he cried and refused to let me go. It was…really hard."

Before Seth could offer sympathy, she set down her fork and lifted her chin. "Can we get this over with? I have to get Jacob ready for bed, and fold laundry, and—"

"I get it," he said gruffly. *We are not friends.* "You said you lived in Hollywood."

"North Hollywood," she corrected.

"Okay." He leaned back. "Were you still married then?"

She became very still, only her eyes vividly alive. Before he could prod her, though, she exclaimed, "What difference does it make?"

"I need to know you if I'm to find out what connects you and Andrea."

"But… I didn't meet her until I arrived here in Lookout." Helen's bewilderment appeared genuine. "If she ever lived in California, she didn't say so to me."

They went back and forth. She didn't want to tell him any specifics. Not her former employer, sure as hell not her ex-husband's name, although she did imply the move here came on the heels of the split from her spouse.

"I don't want any contact with him," she repeated stubbornly.

"Because he might try to take Jacob from you?"

"No!" She tried to sear him with her eyes, but mostly Seth thought she was afraid. "I've already told you all this! He never wanted children. It's me—"

"He didn't want to let you go," he said

slowly, his protective instincts firing up at the very idea of her being terrorized by any man.

"No," she whispered. "At the end, he said he'd kill me if I tried to leave him. I had to get away and hide before I could get legal help to divorce him."

Seth forced himself to take a mental step back. He still couldn't be sure there was a brutal, possessive ex-husband at all. The possibility existed that she was really afraid of *him*, the detective who wouldn't take no for an answer.

"How did you escape him?" he asked.

"I went to a battered women's shelter," she said with such dignity, he felt chastened.

Or was *manipulated* a better word?

Damn, it was hard to hold on to his usual detachment.

"I can check out this man's whereabouts without drawing attention to you. I promise," he said. "All I need is a name."

Helen pressed her lips together and glared at him.

"It doesn't make you even a little nervous that a woman who looks a lot like you was murdered a few days ago here in your kitchen?" He turned in his chair, zeroing in on a stretch of the vinyl floor. "Right about there, if I remember right."

Her gaze followed his, her expression suddenly stricken.

Feeling like a ruthless bastard, Seth waited.

"You don't understand," she said softly.

He kept his own voice quiet. "But I want to."

Her eyes met his, so much hurt in them he dreaded seeing.

"I can't take a chance. I just can't."

The flat finality of her statement had him studying her. What was really going on here? The battered-woman scenario worked in some ways, but not in others. It took a strong woman to tell a detective to his face that she wasn't going to cooperate in his investigation. She had no trouble ordering him to get out when she'd had enough.

And yet, he did believe she was genuinely afraid. Of something.

After a minute, he nodded. "I'll leave you in peace, then." He paused. "For tonight."

Her eyes dilated.

"Helen, you *can't* keep your secrets from me. You might as well resign yourself. I'll find out what I need to know, one way or another."

Pale as a ghost, eyes huge and dark, she stared at him as he turned and then left.

When he got outside to his vehicle, he

planted his hands on the roof, let his head fall forward and swore, long and viciously.

He hated the terrified look in her eyes and couldn't help wondering why he had gone into law enforcement.

ON TIPTOE, ROBIN stretched to reach for a box on the shelf closet, the one that held her few precious mementos. It was stupid to risk so much for them, she knew that, but recovering even this little bit would feel like a victory, a step toward regaining her dignity. She wasn't the pathetic creature who'd numbly put up with Richard's vicious treatment.

I'm not her. Not anymore.

She managed to get her fingertips to each side of the box and tug gently so that it inched forward.

Two minutes, and she'd be out of here.

The softest of sounds came from behind her, and the hair rose on the back of her neck.

Before she could whirl, hard hands gripped her from behind.

"Here you are, right on time," a man growled. Not Richard. Thank God, not Richard.

She wrenched free but fell to her knees. Furious, scared. *So stupid.* She managed to crawl, throw herself toward the bedroom doorway, but he grabbed her hair and wrenched her head back. A knee in the middle of her back drove Robin to the hardwood floor. She was screaming, still fighting. She twisted enough to sink her teeth into the fleshy part of his hand.

Yelling, he hit her. Momentarily, her vision dimmed, but then she realized the blow had sent her flying toward the bed. Robin kicked behind her, felt her foot connect with some part of her assailant's body. She scrambled almost upright and grabbed the lamp on the bedside table. Not one of the pair *she'd* chosen, of course; Richard had smashed those and replaced them with obscenely expensive art deco metal-and-stained-glass monstrosities.

Heavy. She had barely a second to get a good grip. To spin, applying all the force she could muster. To see the lamp base smash into the man's head. To see the shock on his face, to watch the life leave his eyes, to stand stunned as he crumpled.

Only now did she see that the bloody face *was* her ex-husband's. She shook as she stared down at him. *I killed him.*

But then she heard a creak in the hall outside the bedroom. Someone else was here. With her hands trembling, she could hardly hold on to the lamp, yet somehow she lifted it again as if she were a baseball player stepping up to the plate.

Another creak.

"MOMMY?"

Muddled, Helen shot up in bed. It wasn't Richard there that night. It wasn't. So why did she always see his dead face?

Shaking off the sticky web of sleep, she focused on the small shape hovering beside the bed. *Jacob.*

She couldn't let her little boy see her crying. Oh, God. She pulled up her covers and wiped her cheeks, although she still tasted the salt of tears.

"Jacob? What's wrong?"

"I heard scary sounds." His voice sounded... soggy. As if he was crying, too.

"Oh, honey! I'm sorry." She must have cried out in her nightmare. *Please don't let me have actually screamed.* Helen sat up, but didn't turn on the lamp as she usually would have. Instead, she bent to scoop him up and snuggled them both beneath the covers, where it was warm and felt safe, if only she never slept again, never dreamed. "Better?" she murmured against his head.

"My room is scary," he mumbled.

"Just for tonight, you can sleep with Mommy," she murmured. "Okay?"

His head bobbed and he burrowed into her, his knees digging into her stomach. Helen felt another sting of tears at the joy of holding his small, compact body tight. She hadn't known it was possible to love another person so much. The scariest thing in her world was the idea of losing him.

"Sleep tight," she whispered, softly stroking his back until his breathing slowed and his muscles went lax.

Her recurring nightmare was always so vivid, so real…except for the twist at the end. A shameful part of her wished it *was* Richard she'd killed, instead of his butler-bodyguard. He was a monster. Instead, she was haunted by the slack face of a man she hardly knew.

She stiffened. If Detective Renner had entered her fingerprints in that FBI database, he'd know who she was, that she was a person of interest in a previous murder. Why hadn't he? Or had he?

Her teeth wanted to chatter, but she clenched them. She had to take off soon, before it was too late.

Chapter Five

Helen awakened to the peculiar sensation of bobbing as if she were in a small boat riding the wake of a bigger one. With a groan, she pried open her eyes to see Jacob jumping up and down on her bed. His diaper had overflowed, which explained the strong smell of urine. He hadn't yet noticed she'd opened her eyes.

If she felt dazed, it was with surprise because she'd slept, after all. And hadn't had another nightmare, or at least didn't remember one.

Her brain began to resume functioning. This was Saturday. Usually she welcomed the weekends. Even though she had to do errands, she also had time to do fun things with Jacob. Today, she felt weighed down by dread.

Detective Renner would be back to ask more questions. She had to pack without a curious two-year-old *or* a nosy detective noticing. Knowing how much she'd have to leave behind didn't help her mood. Not counting when she first left home for college, this was her third experience of starting entirely over, Jacob's second—but since he'd only been seventeen months old last time, he'd been oblivious to the disruption of sneaking away in the night. This time would be different. It was just as well that he wouldn't understand he'd never see Iris again, or Jenna or bossy Courtney.

Wanting to give him one last day of normalcy, Helen tackled Jacob, but even as she tickled him and laughed along with his giggles, she plotted her day.

Grocery shopping had become a necessity. They'd make it through breakfast, barely, with what remained in the refrigerator and cupboards. Plus she'd need to take some food with them—snacks for Jacob, a small cooler with drinks, breakfasts and probably lunches she could prepare their first days in cheap motel rooms, so they didn't have to waste money eating out, or stop at stores too soon. The less he and she were noticed, the safer they'd be.

Helen hated that she couldn't let Jenna know Jacob wouldn't be coming back, and that they didn't dare say goodbye to her or

Iris. Her mother would describe it as stealing away into the night like thieves.

With sadness that might even be grief, she was dismayed to see Seth Renner's face in her mind's eye, too, as if he were part of what she hated to leave behind. Given the way he'd been questioning her, that made zero sense. Even so, she didn't like knowing that he'd probably think she'd fled because she *had* killed Andrea and feared his investigation.

The disconcerting part was a suspicion he'd also be at least a little hurt because she'd disappointed him, hadn't trusted him. Because he'd never know what had become of her and Jacob.

He'd let her see something she'd never have. As she put together breakfast and then showered quickly, she kept remembering not only the relentless questioning but also the detective's patience and occasional kindness. His smiles for Jacob, the oddly tender note she heard a few times in his voice—the heat in his eyes when he let down his formidable guard. He'd reminded her of what some people were lucky enough to find.

Except, it couldn't possibly be Seth himself she would miss. What she felt was a foolish wish not to be so entirely on her own, that's all.

She'd forget him in no time, except as one more threat, another person who might be tracking her.

THE DAY FELT like summer when Helen ushered Jacob out the front door for the grocery expedition. He immediately cried, "Iris!"

Helen turned to see her neighbor returning from the curb with her newspaper.

Iris waved enthusiastically. "Where are the two of you off to?"

With Jacob, Helen crossed her own somewhat scruffy lawn onto Iris's manicured one. She wrinkled her nose. "Grocery shopping, what else? But since I have to go, is there anything I can pick up for you?"

"Oh, if you wouldn't mind, I forgot eggs when I went to the store yesterday." She smiled at Jacob. "Perhaps this young man would like to stay with me while you do whatever you need to. I thought I'd do a little weeding out back, and I have a plastic bucket and shovel, you know. He can help me."

When she chuckled, Helen had to join her even as her heart ached. Oh, she'd miss Iris. "You're a saint," she declared. She'd have had to say no if Iris had intended to work on her front flower beds, but in back…that ought to be safe enough.

One more thing to hate: how often she used that word in her thoughts. *Safe*.

It was a relief to be able to set off on her own to make another ATM withdrawal and do her shopping. She took her time, calculating what meals would be most practical to make on the run. At last, she went to Walgreen's and bought several modestly priced new toys that should entertain Jacob during days of driving. She'd leave those in the trunk so they'd be a surprise.

She parked, took the groceries into the house and put away everything that had to go in the refrigerator, then slipped out her back door carrying the carton of eggs for Iris. No fence separated their yards.

Iris and Jacob must be inside, leaving the bright blue plastic bucket and yellow shovel on the grass, and a real shovel left standing in what would be a small vegetable garden.

She had started across the yard, when the screen door slammed open, bouncing against the side of the house. A dark figure burst out. In a shocked instant, Helen realized the man wore a ski mask, and had Jacob slung over his shoulder.

With a scream of rage, she dropped the eggs, grabbed the shovel and tore across the lawn to intercept the man who held her sobbing, struggling child. His head swung toward her at the last minute. In a horrible replay of her nightmare, she swung the shovel with all her strength. This time she went for his shins.

He tried to dodge. The blow was glancing, but enough to send him staggering. In that moment, Helen threw herself at him, closing her hand around Jacob's kicking leg even as her shoulder connected with the man's chest or side. Jacob tumbled from his shoulder and she caught him, staggering back.

She retreated a step, her eyes locked on the furious, slitted eyes not hidden by the mask. Heart thundering, Helen knew he'd overpower her easily. She should have held on to the shovel.

She took another step back. He advanced… and they both heard the wail of an approaching siren no more than a few blocks away.

He broke away and ran, disappearing around Iris's detached garage and down the alley, the slap, slap of his footsteps receding.

With a dry sob, Helen sank to the grass, cradling Jacob. She had him. *Thank you, God.*

THE SECOND HE heard Iris Wilbanks's address over the police radio, Seth switched on his lights and siren and accelerated away from the curb. Yeah, this was a small town, but he didn't believe in coincidences.

A patrol officer indicated that he was responding. Seth chimed in to say he was on his way, too.

Since he'd been less than half a mile away, he pulled up in front of Iris's house only seconds behind Officer Todd. He leaped out. His gaze went to Helen's house, but the drawn blinds didn't even twitch.

"I'll go around back," he said tersely, and Todd nodded. As Seth rounded the house, he heard a solid knock on the front door and the young officer calling, "This is the police! I'm coming in."

He felt a torrent of anger and relief and probably more at the sight of Helen sitting in the middle of the yard clutching her sobbing boy. Her fear hit him hard. He'd seen the same expression on the faces of parents who'd had a child go missing, or be hit by a car after running into the street. The knowledge that the unimaginable loss might have happened.

He wasn't even aware of crossing the lawn, only that he crouched beside Helen. However much he wanted to take her and Jacob in his arms, he had to do his job. "Was somebody here?"

"He went that way." She pointed past the garage. "I heard him running down the alley."

"How long ago?"

"Only…only a minute or two."

Seth sprinted, despite knowing he'd be too late. Gun in hand, he reached the side street, where he saw no movement at all…but heard the receding engine of a car.

He ran to the closest house. No one home. The one across the street, the kids were watching cartoons and nobody had seen anything.

Ten minutes later, he walked back to Iris Wilbanks's house to find the backyard empty. He opened the screen door and followed the voices inside.

A pair of paramedics had the woman on a stretcher and were obviously ready to transport her. She was conscious but looked bad, tiny and fragile. Bandages were wrapped her head, and an oxygen mask covered her face.

A distraught Helen stood at her side, Jacob on her hip. "You saved him. I'll never forget. Thank you."

"Ma'am, we need to go," one of the EMTs said.

"Yes." Helen squeezed the older woman's hand and stepped back. Then she saw Seth and came to him, as if it was the most natural thing in the world.

"Hey, buddy," he murmured.

Jacob kept blubbering, and who could blame him? Even if the piece of scum hadn't actually gotten a hand on the boy, he must have seen unfamiliar violence.

"I need to sit down," Helen said suddenly.

He allowed himself to wrap a supportive arm around her as he steered her to the sofa. She sank down as if her knees had given way. Seth excused himself, and he and Dave Todd stepped onto the front porch, both watching as the ambulance pulled away.

"Were you able to talk to the victim?"

"She kept saying, 'Jacob, Jacob,' over and over again."

"That's the boy's name," Seth said. "Okay, let's get the story from Ms. Boyd. She lives next door." He nodded toward her house. "Last week's murder happened in her rental. She tells me she left behind an abusive ex. I'm thinking the two crimes have to be related."

Todd nodded, and the two men went back into the living room. Seth sat on the coffee table facing Helen, while Todd chose a wing chair a little farther away. Fortunately, Jacob's sobs had dwindled to rhythmic snuffling.

"All right," Seth said, "can you tell us what happened?"

"Iris offered to watch Jacob while I grocery

shopped. She said he could help her work on her vegetable garden." She almost sounded steady. "I came home, took my groceries into the house and went out the back door with a carton of eggs for Iris."

Seth could just imagine how much help a two-year-old would have been.

"They weren't outside, though," she continued. "I was partway across the yard when the screen door slammed open and a man wearing a ski mask ran out. He—" her voice broke "—he had Jacob over his shoulder." Her desperate gaze met Seth's. "If I'd been twenty seconds later—"

He couldn't help himself. He reached out and took her hand in his, not surprised to find her fingers were icy. "You weren't."

After a minute, she nodded.

"How did you get Jacob away from him?"

She told them about having noticed the shovel, snatching it up and swinging at the kidnapper's legs. The stumble, her tackle.

"He took off because he heard the approaching siren." Helen shivered. "Iris must have called 9-1-1."

"She did," Todd confirmed.

"She saved Jacob. And she got hurt so badly doing it. I should never have left him with her. Never!"

Out of the corner of his eye, Seth saw the other officer's brows rise, not only at what she'd said, but also the passion in her voice.

His fingers tightened on her hand. "Helen." He waited until he had her full attention. "Was this your ex-husband?"

She shook her head slowly, some bewilderment showing. "No. He was bulkier than Richard. Anyway, I saw his eyes. They were light colored. Gray, I think. Richard's are brown."

"Is your ex-husband the kind of man who'd send someone else to snatch his son for him?"

She didn't hesitate. "Yes."

So he either had scumbag friends or money to hire some muscle.

"All right," he said. "Give me a minute, and then I'll walk you and Jacob home."

Dave Todd followed him outside.

"File a report with what you know," Seth said. "I'll head over to the hospital to talk to Mrs. Wilbanks. With a little luck, she got a better look at the guy."

"You're thinking Ms. Boyd's ex-husband is behind this?"

"If somebody had grabbed the boy when he was momentarily alone, I'd be more likely to consider other possibilities. But to attack openly like this? Assault a woman to get at the kid? Yeah, I think Jacob's father has to be behind it."

"And the murder." Gravity aged Dave Todd's boyish face.

"That, too."

They exchanged a few more words before Todd got back in his patrol car. Going back into the house, Seth asked, "Ready?"

"Yes, of course, but you don't need to—"

He cut her off. "I do."

Helen bit her lip, nodded and started to push herself up. With reaction setting in, she collapsed back onto the cushion. Seth reached for the boy. "I'll carry him."

"If you'll just help me up…"

He waggled his fingers. Jacob looked at him shyly from red, puffy eyes, then took his thumb from his mouth and held up his arms. Seth lifted him, holding him close. "Good boy. Mommy had a tough day."

Helen stood, expression mulish. "And yet, somehow I've always managed fine before."

"Today you don't have to."

She got all the way to the front door before stopping suddenly. "Wait. Iris won't have her insurance card or her keys."

"Good thought. Can you find them? I'll lock the back door while you're looking."

He bent over so Jacob could push the button

on the doorknob. That wouldn't keep an eight-year-old kid out. Dismayed, Seth decided to pick up a dead-bolt lock and install it himself before the home owner was released from the hospital.

Helen handed over both the key and the Medicare Advantage card, waiting on the porch while he locked the door. They'd started along the sidewalk when she exclaimed, "Oh, no! I dropped her eggs. I should go—"

Seth put his free hand on her lower back and gently propelled her forward. "There's no urgency. I feel sure Iris will be admitted to the hospital for the night, at least."

Helen seemed to stumble over her pride when he offered to go get them all hamburgers and fries, but reluctantly accepted.

"Let me walk through your house first," he suggested.

"Please," she said simply.

He hadn't expected that the creep would have circled around and let himself into her place to wait, but had to be sure, checking under her bed and in their closets before feeling satisfied enough to leave.

A local burger restaurant had no drive-through but better quality food, so he went there. As he waited for the order, an uneasy feeling crept over him. He didn't like Helen and Jacob being unprotected even for half an hour, although he honestly didn't expect a repetition of the attack so quickly. And maybe that wasn't even what worried him right now. Helen had to know her ex wasn't going to give up, so what would she do?

He had a suspicion he knew.

IT HADN'T BEEN easy getting rid of Seth, but he did finally leave.

Even on the front porch, he'd turned to give her one last piercing look. "You have to tell me who this guy is. You know that, don't you?"

Knowing she was lucky he'd been patient this long, she said in a small, cracked voice, "Tomorrow."

"All right," he said, sounding astonishingly gentle. "Get some rest, Helen. I'll have patrols drive by regularly this afternoon and during the night. Keep your phone handy. Do you still have my card?"

She nodded.

"Put my number in your phone. If something happens, call 9-1-1 first, then me. Okay?"

"Yes." She felt her smile wobble. "You've been…really nice. Thank you."

He smiled ruefully, not moving. All he did was study her face for longer than was comfortable. Finally, he gave his usual clipped nod and walked down her concrete walkway toward his car. A lump in her throat, Helen watched him go, thinking that even when he appeared relaxed, he wasn't; his head kept turning so he could take in his surroundings, and she suspected he could hit a dead run in about one stride.

And if all went well, she'd never see him again.

When she put Jacob down for his nap, he conked out instantly. Helen hoped all the excitement today had worn him out enough so he'd sleep longer than usual. In case he didn't, she had to hustle.

She'd wait until dark before she went out to the garage to get the two bags she always kept packed. For now, she'd have to revert to her previous identity and pray it wouldn't occur to Richard that she might do that.

Selecting carefully what they could take, she packed everything in a couple of black plastic garbage bags. She openly carried those out to the car under the theory that anyone watching would think she planned to drop them off at the thrift store or maybe the waste disposal site. Nonperishable food went into a cardboard box and grocery bags that she wouldn't take out until after dark.

Midafternoon, Jacob still not having stirred,

she called the hospital, where she was told Mrs. Wilbanks would be spending the night but was responsive and talking. The receptionist put the call through to Iris's room, but nobody answered.

When she tried again after dinner, she was able to talk to Iris, whose first words were "Oh, my dear! Jacob must have been so scared. I didn't do a very good job taking care of him, did I?"

"You did a fabulous job," Helen said firmly. "We saved him because you slowed that awful man down and called 9-1-1 immediately. I got home in the nick of time, but what made him take off was the approaching sirens. I am… so grateful to you, Iris. Losing Jacob—" For a moment she couldn't speak, but knew she didn't have to tell Iris, of all people, what she felt.

The older woman had two adult children, both male, one living in Boston, the other in a Portland suburb, but she'd once confided that her daughter had died from childhood leukemia when she was ten. She and Helen had sat side by side holding hands for several minutes.

Iris was the closest thing Jacob had ever had to a grandmother.

After calming her now, Helen asked how she was feeling, and was unsurprised to hear about a headache. "A concussion, the doctor said," Iris concluded. "I'll look ghastly for a while, too. My left eye is almost entirely swollen shut, and I'm going to have a whopper of a black eye. My jaw hurts, too. I might have lost some teeth, so it's lucky I don't have any." She sounded almost cheerful. "My dentures are intact, thank goodness."

"You're a brave woman, and I'm luckier than I deserve to have you for a neighbor."

Usually Iris would have demurred, but this time she said with satisfaction, "I'll have to call both boys tonight and tell them all about it."

Helen said tentatively, "Did you get a good look at your attacker?"

"I'm afraid not. The detective came to see me earlier, you know. He was so nice. I'm sorry I couldn't help. I heard footsteps—he came in the back door, you see—but I had only started to turn when something slammed into my head. It might have just been his arm, or fist."

"Just?"

Iris chuckled, then moaned. "Oh, I shouldn't do that!"

"I'm sorry—"

"Don't be silly. Jacob ran, you know. I crawled for the phone, and had already dialed 9-1-1 before he got his hands on Jacob and tore out."

Helen hated the image of Jacob trying to run away.

She thanked Iris several more times.

After setting down the phone, Helen stayed where she was at the kitchen table, wrestling again with her conscience. But in the end, what choice did she really have?

None. If she told Seth everything, she risked going to prison and leaving Jacob to Richard's mercy. No. She had to do this.

With a sigh, she took out her checkbook to verify that she'd paid all of her bills, and tucked the latest bank statement into her purse. She'd stop at an ATM wherever she found herself after midnight and take out more money. From that point on, she wouldn't dare use her debit card again. She'd be leaving close to five hundred dollars in the account, but that couldn't be helped. Worse come to worst, she could call her mother and beg for a loan—although she hated doing that.

No, she had enough to take care of them for a few weeks, until she could stop long enough to put together a new identity. Good-bye, Helen, hello… Who knew? Whoever that woman was, she'd have light brown hair,

Helen had already decided. Blond was too memorable. Her natural color was out.

Once Jacob had gotten up from his nap, Helen did her absolute best to keep him from guessing that anything was about to change. She played a game with him, helped him build with his plastic blocks, even watched a Disney movie with him after dinner. Tucked him in, set her alarm and went to bed herself, hoping she could sleep but failing.

At midnight, she got up, packed the last few things—including the connecting blocks—and slipped out to the garage with a flashlight. Shuddering, she had to shake a big spider off one of the duffel bags before she could lift them from hiding and carry them out to stow in the trunk of her car. The remaining packaged food in the kitchen went in the trunk, too. She closed it as quietly as she possibly could, and looked around for any movement in the darkness. Her skin prickled with her nerves, and her chest ached with regret she tried to shake off.

Last was the ice chest, which would ride on the back seat next to Jacob.

She hadn't turned on her porch light, of course. Her eyes had adjusted some to the darkness, but she still had to watch her feet carefully so she didn't trip on the front steps.

That was why she'd almost reached the car before she saw the tall man leaning against the back fender, arms crossed.

He shook his head. "Not happening."

Chapter Six

Seth straightened, took the ice chest from her and inclined his head toward the house. Without a word, Helen turned and retraced her steps.

Inside, he set the ice chest down on the kitchen counter. Face pinched, she'd gotten only as far as the doorway.

"You've been spying on me."

"I have."

"How did you know…?"

There was no easy answer to that. "You only had a few alternatives. I could tell you weren't going to open up to me." He shrugged. "There was something about the way you thanked me." As if she was really saying goodbye.

She wrung her hands together and pleaded, "Please let me go. Richard won't give up. He'll keep coming after me."

"You?" He cocked an eyebrow. "Or his son?"

He lost sight of her shocked stare when she gave an anguished cry and spun to present her back to him.

"Helen." Seth went to stand right behind her. He hesitated before setting his hands on her shoulders and gently squeezing. "Let me help you."

He had no idea whether she saw him as anything but the detective who'd become a major obstacle. Until her secrets were laid bare, he couldn't let himself feel more. She sparked something powerful in him, though. His one certainty was that he needed to keep her close where he could protect her and her son.

With his hands still on her, Seth felt the shuddery breath she drew. "I didn't want to go," she said, so quietly he just heard her. "But I'm scared to stay."

"You have to talk to me, Helen."

The quivering tension in her body relented, and her shoulders sagged. Finally she nodded and, as his hands fell away, faced him. "You haven't left me any choice."

No, he hadn't.

Once she sat at the kitchen table, he pulled out a chair and did the same. "Jacob asleep?"

"I was going to wake him last thing." Her eyes looked more like bitter chocolate than caramel right now.

He couldn't afford much sympathy. "Where did you live before you came to Lookout? You must know I haven't found any background on you before you moved here."

"We did live in Southern California. I told you the truth about that. The thing is…" She looked away, then back to his face, the jut of her chin defiant. "I changed my name."

"I didn't find a divorce decree."

"It wasn't in this state, and… I mean, I did legally go back to my maiden name after the divorce, but later when I had to run, I took on a new identity. When he found me in LA, I did it again. I wasn't Helen Boyd until the day I left."

Well, damn. He'd suspected as much, but taking on new identities wasn't easy these days. "Who were you before?"

"Um… I was Megan Cobb. She… I found her in a cemetery in Seattle. She died before her first birthday." Once again Helen averted her face. "I felt like I'd stolen something." She swallowed. "I did."

"And Helen?"

"Her grave is in Bakersfield, California. She was eight when she died."

Her voice held pity for children who hadn't had a chance to grow up, for their parents, too, but also sharp regret because stealing those identities hadn't kept her and Jacob safe, after all.

"How long had you been in Southern California?" he asked.

"A year and a half. Jacob was born there."

"How did you know your ex-husband had found you?" Seth wondered if she realized she was clutching herself.

"Over several days, I kept seeing the same man. Just glimpses. At the grocery store, near the bus stop I rode to work. The one that wasn't far from Jacob's day care. That time—" she rocked slightly "—he was pointing a camera at me. One with a huge lens."

"What did you do?" Seth couldn't help hearing the growl in his voice.

She seemed calmed by his anger. "I got off the bus at my office, went in like I always do but slipped out through the parking garage. Took a couple of different buses until I got home. I threw a few things in a suitcase, picked up Jacob and just started driving."

"To Bakersfield."

"Yes. I'd decided to stay off major freeways."

"And then you headed toward home."

She chewed on her bottom lip for a minute before her desperate gaze met his. "That might have been stupid, I don't know. I thought it was the last thing Richard would expect."

"The question is how he found you in the first place. And whether he did."

"Why would anyone else be watching me? Or hire an investigator?"

Seth shrugged his concession then grilled her. Had she maintained any hobbies from when she was married?

No. She looked at him like he was nuts. How was a single, working mother of a baby supposed to have *time* for hobbies?

What about work? Was she doing the same kind of jobs she'd had when married, or before her marriage?

Richard hadn't let her work outside the home. His insistence was her first clue that a trap was closing on her. And no, she'd worked in community development with a specific focus on Seattle's problem with a growing homeless population.

"That's how I met him." Her fingernails appeared to be biting into her upper arms. "He— I spoke to the city council. He talked to me afterward."

It was all Seth could do to tamp down his reaction. "Tell me about your family."

"My father died over five years ago, from

a heart attack. It's just Mom, me and my sister, Allie."

"How much contact do you have?"

"Very little. I don't know what can be traced, and what can't. Once in a while, I buy one of those cheap phones, call and then throw it away. That's it."

"Do you always call your mother? Your sister?"

"No. I alternate, and Mom still has a landline, too, so sometimes I use that one."

"Okay." He rolled his shoulders to stretch tight muscles. Here was the part he was really going to hate. "Tell me about your marriage."

THE FIRST WORDS that came out of Helen's mouth were "I was stupid." Even before Seth shook his head, she wished them unsaid. She knew better. She was a smart, educated woman who'd read about abusive relationships and how manipulative, power-mad men wrapped their coils slowly around their prey. Like dipping a toe in cold water, then going ankle-deep, thigh-deep—at which point she'd known she was in trouble—but getting out wasn't so easy once she plunged into the icy depths.

"What happened is on *him*," he said.

"Yes. Yes, it is," Helen agreed fiercely. The

counseling she'd received while in the women's shelter had helped her recover her confidence. For her, it happened fast, because she'd escaped her marriage quickly. It hadn't lasted even two years.

"Why did you fall for him?"

She gazed at a bare stretch of wall so that she didn't have to see what Seth was thinking.

Voice tight, she said, "He's handsome, maybe the most intelligent person I'd ever met, seemingly committed to a lot of good causes. He...has this sort of force field. I guess it's charisma, but once people are sucked in, they want him to like them. They tend to do what he suggests, too."

"Sounds like a warlock."

"Yes. I never figured out if he really is well-intentioned in his stances on issues. Maybe I satisfied his need for control while he had me." She hated feeling shame, didn't deserve to feel it, but that was a battle she hadn't entirely won yet. "It was classic. He didn't want me to work, always thought of something the two of us could do when I planned to get together with a friend or Mom or Allie. His intensity kept me from noticing. I thought this sort of passionate closeness was normal in the first year of marriage." She meant to laugh, but the sound was discordant. "Then he started giving me the silent treatment if I displeased him, which was awful since half the time I had no idea what I'd done or said. The first time he hit me, I almost left him, but he groveled, and I was sure I'd provoked his temper, and..." Her muscles rigid, she hadn't moved since she'd started talking. "Only then it happened again. And again. I made up my mind to leave him. Unfortunately, the housekeeper called to let him know I was packing to go, and he came home. He beat me so badly, he had to take me to the ER. I think the doctor there suspected, but I made up some story because Richard was sitting there holding my hand, so loving and solicitous. After that, he told me no woman left him, and if I tried, he'd kill me. That made me wonder—" She hesitated.

"About?"

"He'd been married before, to a woman he met when he was a graduate student at the University of Michigan. She'd died in some kind of accident, supposedly."

Seth said something she was just as glad not to hear.

"I was essentially a prisoner from then on. The housekeeper lived in, and a man started work as sort of a butler but really more of a bodyguard—and prison guard. After that, no matter how careful I was, I couldn't please Richard. I made visits to half the emergency rooms in the city. He kept entertaining with me as his hostess, but he made sure I never had a chance to be alone with any of the guests." She let out a long breath. "I'm not sure I'd have had the nerve to latch onto someone I didn't know very well and beg for rescue, anyway."

"But you did escape." Seth's voice was guttural.

"Yes. I waited for a chance when no one was watching. I'd been stealing a little bit of money at a time from Richard. He'd drop his coins or a few dollars on the dresser at night. You know." Her shrug had to look as stiff as it felt. "I didn't need much. When I saw my chance, I walked out. No coat, I couldn't take anything. I…had bruises on my face. I walked quite a way before I saw a taxi. When I got in, the taxi driver took one look at me, then drove me to a hospital. A social worker called a women's shelter for me. Someone came to get me." She stopped.

"You were pregnant."

Helen turned her head slowly to look at him. His face remained impassive, but his eyes glittered with what she knew was fury. Seeing that let her relax a little. It comforted her.

"I had been feeling tired and nauseated for several weeks, but I thought it was stress. Thank God I left when I did." The alternative still horrified her. "He had no idea I was pregnant."

Seth leaned forward. "Do you have scars?"

"I… Only a couple. He…mostly broke bones."

Muscles in the detective's jaw clenched. His blue eyes burned into hers. "Will you show me?"

Startled, she shrank back. "Show you?"

"Your scars."

He needed proof, she supposed. After a moment, she nodded.

His chair scraped back. Bending her head, she tugged the collar of her sweatshirt aside so he could see the spot low on her neck.

"He sometimes smoked cigars. Expensive Cuban ones, of course. He sort of stabbed me with the burning tip of one."

Her fingers could have unerringly found the scar, even though the skin there no longer felt any sensation. Still, she'd swear she felt Seth lightly touch it with the tip of his finger.

"I have a couple of other places, but I'd have to take clothes off, and I…" Her cheeks felt hot. She didn't want to strip in front of him, for a whole lot of reasons.

"Okay." He gently tugged the neckline of her shirt back up. She could hear him breathing behind her. What was he doing? But then he returned to his place at the table, his expression grim. Helen knew what was coming.

"What's his name, Helen?" He frowned. "What's *your* name?"

Panic skittered over her. "You can't—"

"I can't what?"

"I don't know!" she exclaimed. It was obvious Richard already knew where she was. "I just—"

He waited.

Was there any chance at all he could ask questions about Richard without learning about the bodyguard's murder?

She closed her eyes in resignation. What could she do but tell him? At least for now, running wasn't an option. The knowledge gave her a claustrophobic feeling.

Possibly because she was, once again, trapped? Another man had seized control over her life? Yes. Dear God, *yes*.

And yet…relief was part of what she felt, too. She hadn't wanted to leave this life and people she'd come to care about behind. Surrendering the burden of responsibility, if only briefly, that was a relief, too.

Unless, of course, she ended up being arrested.

Unreadable, Seth kept watching her.

"Richard Winstead. He's…a corporate attorney in Seattle. He sits on several advisory committees appointed by the mayor and city council members." Bitterness etched her voice when she added, "If you ask around about him, all you'll hear are glowing compliments."

"He's not the first successful man to abuse his wife. Domestic violence covers every social class."

She swallowed and nodded. "I'm Robin Hollis."

Seth's smile reached his eyes. It was warm and a little crooked. "Thank you, Robin." He resumed his cop mask. "Here's what we're going to do first. If you'll give me permission, I think we should compile your medical records."

Stung, she said, "You don't believe me." Except… Confused, she realized he'd said "we." Twice. As if *they* were taking action, not just him.

"I do," he said calmly. "It would help to show undeniable proof to a judge that you suffered not just one incident but ongoing abuse at the hands of your then-husband. The dates of your visits to the various ERs are important. I won't be surprised if doctors or nurses noted some suspicion of abuse, too."

She'd thought of requesting her records herself, but had been afraid to give a mailing address to the various hospitals. To have them sent to her mother might have drawn attention to her. One of her fears had always been what Richard might do to Mom and Allie to punish her.

"Yes. I'll sign a permission form."

"Good. We'll start with that." He tapped the ice chest. "Might be a good idea to put everything in here back in the fridge."

Suddenly exhausted, she pushed herself to her feet while she still could and lifted off the lid. "I need to get some things from the car, too. My toothbrush is out there."

"Do you have to brush your teeth?"

She blinked at him. Did she really care? No. "I suppose not."

Shaking his head, he stood. "You need to get to bed. I'll put the food away."

"But…"

"I'm sleeping on your couch tonight, Robin."

"To keep me from taking off once you're gone."

He smiled. "I admit the thought crossed my mind that you might try, but I want you to get a good night's sleep, too, and I know you won't if you're listening for a break-in."

He was right. A part of her had been dread-ing his departure. She felt guilty, though. This had to be above and beyond the call. Could he get in trouble for staying in her house?

"If I promise—" she began.

Seth shook his head. "Go to bed, Robin."

"It's weird hearing my name."

He put his hands on her shoulders, turned her toward the living room and gave her a nudge. "Sleep tight."

She almost smiled at hearing that. Mom always said the same when she'd tucked her daughters into bed. "There's an extra pillow and some blankets in the linen closet."

"I'll be fine."

She went, afraid she'd still lie awake wondering about the consequences of her telling him so much. She peeked in at Jacob, as she always did before going to bed herself, closed her own door while she shed her clothes, then cracked it open again to allow her to hear Jacob. Bedside light off, she crawled into bed and conked out.

SETH LAY ON the couch, one shoeless foot on the floor, the other extending beyond the padded arm. Considering that it looked as if she'd bought it at a garage sale, the couch wasn't half bad as a makeshift bed. Just not long enough. That wasn't all keeping him awake, though.

Every time he pictured her buckling Jacob into his car seat and driving away, his guts knotted. If he hadn't listened to his instincts, Helen—no, Robin—would be gone, no question. He wouldn't have gotten her out of his head for a long time.

Mentally replaying her story didn't help, either. It wasn't as if he hadn't seen plenty of domestic abuse during his career; brutality at home was a staple in any patrol officer's job, small town or big city. He'd never been sure how he'd controlled his anger in those situations. He'd never get why a man would want to hurt any woman or child, far less the ones he loved. This time, he already felt more than he should for Helen Boyd aka Robin Hollis. Seeing the scar had fired his temper. Now, when he closed his eyes in search of sleep, he saw her face with lopsided swelling, purple bruises, a swollen eye like Iris Wilbanks's.

Yeah, he sounded capable of being that cold-blooded.

Seth's thoughts kept veering to the woman down the hall. Better not to wonder if she slept on her back or curled on her side, if she'd gravitate toward the warmth of a man sharing her bed. Hard to stop himself, though. Hard not to wish he'd seen more than glimpses of the woman she'd been before she got sucked into the orbit of a monster.

Her choice of profession before her marriage suggested that compassion was a big part of her makeup. That hadn't changed; all he had to do was remember her kneeling beside her injured neighbor, holding her hand.

He tried to push away the memory of her saying she'd been tired and nauseated for only a few weeks before she escaped. She had to have hated the SOB by the time she got pregnant. Had she been cooperating, trying in self-defense to please him, or had he outright raped her whenever he felt like it?

Make sure there really is a Richard Winstead who'd been married to Robin Hollis, Seth cautioned himself. He believed in the anguish he'd seen on her face, but call him a cynic. He still needed to see those doctors' reports and X-rays.

It was a long night despite getting a late start. He got up to use the bathroom once, pausing in the hall after turning out the light to look in the narrow slot of darkness that was her bedroom. He wished he could see her, know whether she'd actually been able to sleep.

He did finally drop off, but the sleep was

light. He jerked awake at regular intervals, thinking he'd heard something, lying still listening until he was sure he hadn't. The deepest sleep must have come toward morning, because he opened his eyes to find a short person staring at him from less than a foot away. He had to blink to bring the caramel-brown eyes, disheveled red hair and freckles into focus. His nostrils flared at the distinct smell of pee.

"Hi," the little boy said engagingly.

"Good morning." Seth had to clear his throat. "Do you need a bath?"

Jacob's head bobbed.

"How about a shower?"

His eyes widened in alarm, and he shook his head hard.

Okay, Seth remembered a time when he'd been terrified of getting water in his eyes or mouth, too.

"Mommy awake?" he tried.

Another headshake.

Well, this would be a first for him, but why not?

Chapter Seven

Waking to the sounding of water running and a huge *splat*, Helen shot upright in bed. Dear God, Jacob hadn't turned the tub faucet on himself, had he?

She sprang out of bed and raced toward the bathroom, but before she reached it, she heard the low rumble of a man's voice, then Jacob's giggle. She stopped dead in the hall, gaping at the open bathroom door. Seth Renner—*Detective* Renner—was giving her son a bath? Had he tried to wake her up and failed? What time was it anyway?

She retreated to her bedroom and sat on the edge of the bed so she could see her clock: 8:56. Since Jacob was usually awake by 6:30, she couldn't remember the last time she'd slept this late.

She threw on her robe—terry cloth and not a thing of beauty—and padded across the hall to the bathroom.

"Mommy!" Jacob cried joyously. He started to scramble to his feet, but Seth laid a hand on his skinny shoulder and shook his head.

"Sit, buddy. You don't want to slip and fall." Then he turned his head and smiled at Helen. Sitting on a plastic stool she'd bought for the express purpose of supervising baths, he wore the same khaki trousers, and a white T-shirt he must have had under the button-up she remembered from last night.

What riveted her attention was his bare feet.

Big feet, to suit his height, a few dark hairs curling on his toes. Solid feet, she thought, for no good reason except she liked them better than Richard's, which had been narrow and fish-white. Not that she had any business liking Seth's feet, or even staring at them.

"My socks got wet," he said. "I didn't realize what a messy business this is."

"Why…?"

"I woke up to find somebody staring at me. He said when he tried to wake up Mommy, she grumbled and rolled over."

"He did not!"

This smile crinkled the skin beside his eyes. "He was happy to discover a second-stringer snoozing on the couch."

She laughed even as she shook her head. "I

can't believe I didn't wake up! What would he have done if you hadn't been here?"

"Well, I don't think he's tall enough to unlock the front door yet, but he might have gotten into the refrigerator."

"I'm hungry," her son declared.

"Me, too." Seth's eyebrows rose.

Jacob bounced. "I want waffles."

Didn't Seth plan to go home today? Imagining him leaving, she felt a spike of anxiety. Yesterday, Richard's minion had tried to steal Jacob in broad daylight. What was to stop him once she and Jacob were alone?

"Waffles it is," she agreed, not quite as lightly as she'd intended. "Except I'd really like to have a shower first."

"I think it's time for Jacob to get out, anyway." Seth grinned at the two-year-old. "You're getting crinkled fingers and toes."

He was, which made her wonder how long he'd been happily splashing and playing in the tub while she slept, oblivious.

"Okay, kiddo." She grabbed his towel from the rack and handed it to Seth. Her hand brushed his, but she pretended she hadn't noticed. "Mommy's turn."

"Mommy's turn," Jacob said obediently. When Seth held out the small plastic bucket that still held a few toys, Jacob put the ones he'd been playing with into it.

Packing yesterday, she hadn't included of bath toys, Helen thought, suddenly stricken. Jacob especially loved his bright red boat and the purple shark.

Seth was watching her, she realized, reading her emotions. She forced a smile. "If you two can handle this, I need to find myself some clean clothes." Some that weren't in the trunk of her car.

Even as she thought that, Seth said, "Do you need me to go out and get something from the car?"

"No, I'm fine. I didn't try to— You know." *Take everything.*

His expression changed, the warmth disappearing, but Seth gave a curt nod.

Helen fled for her bedroom.

SHE'D MADE WAFFLES from scratch. Seth couldn't remember the last time he'd had any that good. She even made him a second waffle. While he ate it, Helen—no, damn it, Robin!—took Jacob down the hall to use his potty chair. The boy didn't seem to need a diaper during the day. Nights must be different.

"He sleeps too soundly," she said with a fond smile for the boy. After rinsing off his plate, Seth found her keys in an outside pocket of her purse and went out to grab the first load from the trunk. Two duffel bags, looking pretty scroungy.

Coming down the hall, she saw what he was carrying. "Oh, those are—" She eyed him warily. "I keep them packed. You know."

"Go bags."

"Something like that," she admitted.

He shook his head. "Should I bring in just the boxes?"

"No, I need the bags, too, but I can help."

"Won't take me a minute." He went back outside before he had to get mad at her again for planning to run out on him.

Once everything was inside, he went into the kitchen, where she was rinsing dishes. "I'm going out to get my laptop," he told her.

"Where are you parked?"

"Alley behind Mrs. Wilbanks's house."

She narrowed her eyes. "Sneaky."

He just smiled. Once he'd returned, he pulled up a list of hospitals and urgent care facilities in King County and when he read it aloud, she identified six places where she'd been treated.

Six. Seth wasn't smiling anymore.

Since this was Sunday, it wouldn't do any good to send off the requests before morning, especially since he'd need her to come into the station to sign a permission form he could scan.

In the meantime, he had no intention of going anywhere. Which was fine today as long as he didn't get called out, a possibility even on his days off. If that happened, he'd have to figure out what to do with Robin and Jacob. He wouldn't leave them unguarded.

Speaking of which... He closed his laptop and said what he was sure were her favorite words: "Let's talk." Seeing her anxiety, he shook his head. "Nothing bad."

"Then what?"

"I don't want you staying here," he said bluntly.

Her mouth tightened. "Then you should have let me go, shouldn't you?"

"I need to know where you are." He hoped she didn't understand how sincerely he meant that.

She only frowned. "I guess I could go back to the Lookout Inn. The security there is probably decent. Better than a bed-and-breakfast."

"But not good enough. You'd be easy to find. It'll be best if you just disappear. We'll leave your car here, slip out the back door during the night."

Now she looked wary. "Where would we go?"

He wished he could take them home—and the force of that desire was good reason to nix the idea. Along with the fact that, unless he took some vacation, she and Jacob would be unprotected while he worked.

"To stay with my father," he said. Although maybe he should have called Dad before proposing this, Seth realized belatedly. "He's a retired cop, has lots of room."

"You're kidding."

"No."

Helen—damn it, he didn't like being so confused—*Robin* shook her head. "We can't descend on your father. I've never even met him! And with a two-year-old…? Have you asked him?" she queried with spot-on suspicion.

"I'll call him right now."

Robin jumped up. "There's got to be someplace else we can go. I've gotten to be friends with one of my coworkers—"

He leaned back in his chair and crossed his arms. "Can she protect you? Does she have family you'd be endangering?"

"Oh, God." She plunked back down onto the chair, looking dazed.

Seth said gently, "I'm sorry, Robin."

Her eyes truly focused then. "Maybe you shouldn't call me that."

"Why not? It's safe to say your ex knows what name you've been living under."

Her mouth tightened.

Seth took out his phone and tapped his father's number. Robin leaped up and said hastily, "I'd better check on Jacob. And let you talk to your dad without me listening in."

"It's okay—"

But she was gone. She was probably right, he thought, just as his father said, "Son?"

"Hey, Dad. Ah, listen, I need to ask a favor of you."

There was a pause. "What is it?"

"I'm looking for someplace for a woman and her toddler son to stay for a few days. She's in a tough spot."

"This somebody you're seeing?"

"No, nothing like that." Did he sound as falsely hearty as he thought he did? "We talked about the Realtor who was murdered. She was killed in a rental house. This woman is the renter. I think Ms. Sloan was killed by mistake. She looked a lot like Ms. Boyd." He caught himself. "Hollis. Crap. She's living here under a false identity to escape an ex-husband."

Silence. He'd worried before about women mixed up in his investigations, but Seth had never put one under his father's protection.

Dad was waiting to hear what this was really about.

"Yesterday, somebody tried to snatch her son. She'd left him for a couple of hours with her next-door neighbor, an older woman named Iris Wilbanks."

"I know Iris," his father put in. "Did she get hurt?"

"The creep knocked her down, so she has a concussion and a black eye. Doctor kept her overnight, but she's coming home today. How'd you meet her?"

"She worked at the library. Nice lady."

"Yeah, she is." Seth sighed and told him how Robin had fearlessly rushed the abductor and gotten her son back. He outlined the rest of her history—the abusive ex, the changed identities, even her attempt to take off again.

"You getting involved with this woman?"

Seth winced. His father knew him too well. "I'm trying not to," he said.

"Why?"

He glanced at the doorway, glad to hear her talking down the hall. Even so, he lowered his voice. "You have to ask? She's involved in my investigation. I can't a hundred percent swear she's telling the truth yet."

"Uh-huh."

"Dad."

"Of course she's welcome." There was a smile in his father's voice. "Won't mind having a kid around the house, either. It's been a long time."

"You had your grandkids for two weeks at Christmas." Seth's sister, Grace, tried to get home with her girls at least twice a year, sometimes with her husband, sometimes not. The bedroom with two single beds Dad kept for the girls would do nicely for Robin and Jacob.

"Why Grace had to marry a man based in Chicago, I don't know."

"Maybe because she went to the University of Chicago," Seth suggested, smiling at his father's oft-heard grumbles.

Robin appeared in the doorway, hesitating when she saw he was still on the phone. He waved her in.

"I want to sneak Robin and Jacob out in the early hours tonight. You don't have to get up. I'll let us in and put them in Ivy and Sara's bedroom."

His father snorted. "You know I won't sleep through that. I'll at least say hello."

"Okay, Dad. Thanks."

He harrumphed. "Maybe I'll see more of you while they're with me."

"I'm sure you will."

Putting his phone down on the table, Seth said, "Dad's glad to have you." He told her about his two nieces, the bedroom she'd share with Jacob, and the wealth of toys and kids' DVDs his father kept around. "He's a good guy."

Her smile was crooked. "So is his son." Pause. "Most of the time."

Seth laughed.

HAVING SETH HANGING around all day was unnerving. Of course, if he hadn't been here, she'd have been so tense she wouldn't have been able to do anything but listen for every tiny creak, or peer through blinds when cars passed in the street or alley. Instead, a big, sexy man had inserted himself calmly into her home, interacting comfortably with Jacob and talking to her as if they were longtime friends. Or lovers.

He did take his laptop out off and on, mostly seeming engaged in doing searches. That made her nervous. He'd find plenty about her under her real name, first because of the work she'd done, then because of her marriage to a prominent man. Was he reading about her parents? And what about her sister? He wouldn't have any reason to track down information about Allie's health problems, would he? *Please, no.*

Of course, Seth would be researching Richard. Robin wished she knew what he was thinking. He looked up frequently, his gaze going straight to her. Clearly, even while he appeared immersed in whatever he was reading or doing, he remained aware of her.

Well, she was aware of him, too. Painfully so. He looked good slouching, feet stacked on the coffee table, or sitting up bent over the laptop. His long fingers, the sinews and veins in his hands mesmerized her, as did the thickness of his wrists, the strength in tanned forearms below rolled shirtsleeves. No matter what she did, she'd find her gaze straying to him—and, most often, his eyes would already be on her.

She gave herself lectures. She couldn't forget that friendship wasn't what had him spending his Sunday here with her and Jacob. He was keeping an eye on her so she wouldn't take off. Yes, and guarding them, too; she couldn't deny that.

What disturbed her most was that by the time she escaped from Richard, she hadn't been able to imagine ever letting a man close enough to hurt her again, emotionally or physically. Her several-month stay in the battered-women's shelter had reinforced her determination. Every woman there was running from a man who'd once promised to love and cherish her but chose instead to use his fists on her—or systematically destroy her confidence. Most had been in damaging relationships much longer than Robin had been, in part because she'd had more confidence to start with and been lucky enough to grow up with parents who were happily married. Her father was often laughing in her memories. He'd had a special glint in his eyes for her mother until the day he died.

Robin felt ashamed, thinking about her father. With him as an example, how could she not have seen beneath Richard's charming surface before she married him?

But she also knew what Dad would say. *You got out of it as quick as you could. You'll for damn sure make sure he never has a chance to hurt your baby.* If Dad had still been alive, she suspected she'd have left Richard much sooner—and gone home instead of hiding out in a shelter.

But Allie hadn't been sick then; in fact, they hadn't known that she had only one kidney. Mom hadn't become worn with worry for both her daughters, the sick one and the one who could so rarely be bothered to call or take time to stop by the house, who invited her mother and sister to dinner at her elegant home only on rare occasions. When, of course, Richard had seen to it that they didn't have time for private conversation. When he'd been at his warmest, funniest, and they, too, had fallen into that force field.

Until Robin had called from the shelter to tell them what her marriage had really been like, they'd undoubtedly thought she was glad to leave them behind for a more glamorous life with a wealthy, politically influential man.

She shook off memories of him when it came time to tuck Jacob in for his nap.

"I like Seth," he said sleepily.

She kissed his still-round cheek and murmured, "I do, too."

She eased the door almost closed and stayed facing it for a minute. Why Seth? Why did he feel…trustworthy? Why was her body all too responsive to him, when she hadn't thought about a man in a sexual way since a year into her marriage?

With a sigh, she returned to the living room.

Wouldn't you know, he looked up immediately, his blue eyes piercing her.

"Come sit down." He patted the cushion next to him.

Her feet quit moving. "Is this going to be another interrogation?"

His mouth curved. "No."

She approached reluctantly, finally sitting beside him. He turned his laptop slightly to allow her to see a photo of Richard engaged in intense conversation with the previous mayor.

"Handsome man," Seth said, tone neutral.

Taken by surprise, Robin couldn't tear her eyes from that face. Lean, his strength wiry, his face thin with perfect bones, a sensual mouth and extremely dark eyes beneath a slash of dark brows.

A shudder racked her. "Looking at him makes my skin crawl."

Seth slapped the laptop closed. "I'm sorry. God! What was I thinking?"

"You...you wanted to know more about him." With each hand, she gripped the opposite forearm, kneading hard.

"Robin." Seth took her hands, prying them away from her arms. "Don't. Please."

She shook her head. "I've been following him on social media and in the news. I wanted to be sure he was in Seattle where he belongs. I've seen pictures before. Tonight... I don't know why it hit me that way."

But she did. It was because of what she'd been thinking, comparing Richard to Seth.

Richard's touch, his cold rebukes, had been cast in sharp relief. She hadn't known she could act until that last year, but she'd hated every minute.

She shivered.

With an exclamation, Seth dropped her hands and pulled her into his arms. Without a second thought, she all but burrowed into him, wrapping her arms around his hard torso.

"I'm sorry," he said roughly. "I think I wanted—" He swallowed.

Robin tried to lift her head. "You wanted?"

"I was being an idiot. Reading about him and thinking—"

He kept doing that. There was something he'd rather not admit.

She struggled back and Seth released her. They were left staring at each other.

"What?" Suddenly mad, she demanded, "What did you think?"

His mouth twisted. "I feel like a country hick in comparison, that's what. I know I'm being illogical. I despise every breath the son of a bitch takes, but I didn't like knowing—" Looking appalled, he closed his mouth and seemed to retreat without seemingly moving a muscle.

Knowing what? She couldn't imagine.

"I can see why he impressed you." Seth was

good at the expressionless thing, except when he almost slipped.

"No. You don't understand." She laid a hand on his arm, which became even more rigid. "I wasn't attracted to his wealth, or the fact that he seemed to have so much influence on a lot of important people. I detested the entertaining he took for granted we'd do, and his house—" She barely controlled another shiver. "We seemed to have so much in common. He listened to me, acted as if he respected my opinions." If the curve of her mouth looked bitter, that was because it was. "Until he suddenly didn't want me working, got mad at any suggestion *he* wasn't enough to satisfy me. Oh, and how dare I counter his brilliant ideas? By then I'd started to wonder if political expedience wasn't his main consideration when he took sides on issues."

Seth didn't say a word, but lines gathered on his forehead.

"I know you're just doing your job." She gestured vaguely, encompassing the sofa where he'd slept last night, the fact that he was still here. "Considering that you must still doubt everything I've told you, you've been kind and protective. Jacob doesn't know many men, but he trusted you immediately.

And you're, well…" No way she could finish *that* sentence.

One eyebrow flickered. "Trustworthy. Kind. Sounds like a nice dog you adopted at the local shelter."

"It's not like that." Seeing his disbelief, she blurted, "He can't measure up to you in any way."

His eyes narrowed slightly. Then he rolled his shoulders and said drily, "At least I don't beat women."

Cheeks warm, Robin mumbled, "You know that's not what I meant."

His eyes had never been so blue. Her heartbeat did some gymnastics while they looked at each other. He wouldn't touch her, she knew he wouldn't, but Robin was shaken to realize how sure she was that he wanted to.

And that she was extraordinarily tempted to take the decision out of his hands.

Chapter Eight

Seth rose abruptly from his place on the couch. "I'm going to take a look around outside."

Sitting in a rocker, Robin had been reading—or pretending to read, just as he'd pretended to be absorbed in the news on his computer. He'd noticed she hurriedly turned a page whenever he glanced her way, and rarely in between. Now she only nodded.

He stalked through the kitchen and utility room. Neither room was lit, and Robin hadn't turned on the porch light, either. It was a very dark night he let himself out into. Clouds had moved in earlier; now, a wind gusted through the alley and backyard. He stepped to one side of the door and waited for his eyes to adjust to the relative darkness.

In town, it was never entirely dark, of course. Halfway down the alley, light poured out of an open garage. Streetlamps stood at corners throughout the neighborhood. But the houses to each side of Robin's were dark. Seth had sent a patrol officer to bring Iris home from the hospital earlier. She must have already gone to bed.

He walked up the alley, then back until he reached the cross street, careful not to let his booted feet crunch on the occasional gravel. Once, movement seen out of the corner of his eye had him tensing, until he saw a cat leap over a six-foot fence. His unmarked department car remained inconspicuously tucked up close to Iris's small, detached garage.

Moving silently, he circled Iris's house, then Robin's rental. Nothing. At nearly nine o'clock, everybody in the neighborhood seemed to be tucked in to stay. He hadn't heard a car engine since he'd come outside, only a few clangs of metal inside that open garage.

Still restless, glad for the cool night air and the distance from a woman he hungered for but couldn't allow himself to touch, Seth wasn't eager to go back inside. Robin might start to worry if he didn't reappear, however. He hoped she'd go to bed soon and get some sleep before their planned getaway. Four a.m. There shouldn't be so much as a mouse astir, and no hint of dawn yet, either.

He'd quietly let himself in and locked the

new dead bolt on the back door when he heard a phone ring. Had to be Robin's. Strange, when nobody had called all day. The only time she'd been on her phone was to talk to Iris once she was home.

Not wanting to scare her, he called, "It's me," and stopped to pour a glass of cold water from the pitcher in the refrigerator.

"Seth?" She was suddenly there, clutching her phone. "It's a strange number."

This was probably innocent: a sales call, a family member using a burner. But threats... those might be next. He set the glass down on the counter. "Answer."

Eyes locked on his, Robin answered after the fifth ring. "Hello?"

All Seth could hear was a man's voice, but her outraged expression told him who this caller was.

"How did you get my phone number? And what do you want?"

The man talked. Seth thought she might crack the phone case, the way her hand had tightened. He had to fight the desire to snatch it out of her grip and tell the son of a bitch what he thought about men who terrorized women.

But she was already talking again. "You're crazy," she said scathingly, stunned disbelief showing, too. "Oh, why am I surprised? Of course you are." The man's voice cut like a whip, but over the top of it, Robin talked right over him, gaining volume as she went. "The answer is no. I already know you don't keep promises. More to the point—" she was almost yelling now "—I would *never* give up my child to anyone, and especially not *you*."

Seth didn't think he'd ever heard so much loathing in anyone's voice.

Apparently having cut the creep off, she dropped the phone onto the table and paced the length of the kitchen and back. "How *dare* he call me? Did he think for a minute that I'd just hand over Jacob? Or was he only goading me?"

When she started past him again, he stopped her with a hand on her arm. "Tell me what he said."

"That he'd let me go if I gave him his son. Signed a note conceding custody to him."

"That's brazen."

"He thinks he's untouchable. Who would believe me if I told them what he'd done to me? What he's really like?"

"I do," Seth said simply.

Her lips parted. She blinked. "I… How can you?"

A little shocked to have said that—no, to

believe in her so absolutely—he shook his head. "Doesn't matter. I wish I could have recorded that call, though. He all but admitted he was responsible for the attempted abduction."

"Yes." Her shoulders slumped. "I hate him."

"Yeah." He sounded hoarse to his ears. He wanted to gather her into his arms, as he had for those brief moments on the couch, but knew he needed to keep his distance. She'd passed the point of being a suspect in his eyes, but starting anything with her was highly inappropriate. No matter what, he couldn't put her in a position of feeling coerced, not when she needed to be able to depend on him. As for him, whatever his gut insisted was truth, he'd be smart to see some proof before he gave Robin Hollis–Helen Boyd–Megan Cobb his entire faith—and maybe the something more that formed a tight knot under his breastbone.

ROBIN'S HEAD KEPT TURNING, although she couldn't make much out in the dark. Beside her in the alley, Seth carried Jacob, who was still half-asleep. A duffel hung over his opposite shoulder, while she carried a box and one of the big black plastic sacks full of clothes.

They'd reached his car when she gasped. "His car seat," she whispered.

"I got it." He eased open the back door and gently placed Jacob in the seat, buckling him in with a deftness that told her he'd done this before. "Slipped out earlier," he murmured. "Brought the potty seat, too. Lucky he didn't need it."

Her lips formed a "thank you." She didn't know if he heard it. The bags all went on the seat and floor by Jacob. Seth urged her into the front passenger seat. "Lock. I'll get the rest."

She did as he asked, watching the side mirror as he melted back into the darkness. With her awareness that they were alone, prickles of apprehension crawled up her spine. What if somebody lunged out of the darkness right now? That man in the mask could break the car window with one smash of a hammer, unlock the back door and have Jacob out before she could do much. A bullet could come out of nowhere and she'd be dead. Richard had sworn more than once that he would kill her if she fled. After she'd rejected the "deal" he proffered today, what was to stop him? For all his liberal stances, he owned a sizable collection of guns, from 9 mm handguns to rifles and worse.

She should have told Seth about Richard's

guns, and that he was an expert marksman. Was Seth armed tonight?

Nothing moved in the darkness. She swiveled to see that Jacob had sagged sideways in deep sleep again. He'd be up bright and early, but she could probably vacuum around his bed in the middle of the night without waking him.

Where was Seth? *Please hurry.*

As if she'd conjured him, a dark shape materialized behind the car. The trunk lid rose without a sound. Seth set his current load inside and eased the lid back down with barely a click that she felt more than heard. She unlocked the doors to let him in.

The minute he was behind the wheel, he locked them in again and started the engine.

"I'll bet he's watching," she said.

Driving slowly down the alley, Seth glanced at her. "Round the clock surveillance is expensive."

"He's rich."

"And conspicuous in a small town like this. You don't think any of your neighbors wouldn't call the police if they saw a guy sitting for hours on end in a car? Or lurking in the alley? Crossing backyards?"

"Yes, but..."

A warm hand covered hers where she clutched the seat belt. "Quit worrying."

"I forgot to tell you that Richard owns guns. He target shoots a couple of times a week."

In a different tone, Seth said, "Does he, now? Did he teach you to shoot?"

"He tried. It didn't go well."

"Why not?" He sounded genuinely interested. They'd exited the alley and were driving down a deserted street.

"It freaked me out. The way the gun leaped in my hand."

"What kind of gun?"

"It was a Beretta M9, he said. Kind of tan colored."

Seth grunted. "Pricey, which figures. Too big for you. If he'd really wanted to teach you, he'd have started with something with less punch and sized for smaller hands."

Had Richard really wanted her to share his hobby? Funny, Robin thought, that she'd never asked herself that question, but in retrospect she thought his goal had been for her to see how deadly *he* was with a weapon in his hands. Precautionary intimidation. If only she'd guessed as much. She'd have become a crack shot if it killed her, scared *him* a little.

Seth drove several blocks before he added, "If somebody were to take a shot at you right about now, he'd be my number one suspect."

"He may not know I've told you about him.

He might think I'm hanging on to my Helen Boyd identity."

"If this works, he won't be able to find you either way. Seems likely he'll assume you've taken off again."

"I have."

He chuckled quietly. "Less than a mile between Dad's house and yours."

They did some zigzagging along the way, Seth keeping an eye on the rearview mirror. Robin compulsively did the same using the passenger-side mirror. They had left town before the car slowed and he turned into a long dirt driveway. There seemed to be an orchard to one side and a pasture to the other.

"Is this where you grew up?"

His hands flexed once on the steering wheel. "Yep. I had a lot of fun here as a kid."

What should pop out of her mouth but "You're... You seemed to know your way around a car seat."

"Is that a question?" He was clearly teasing. "I have two nieces. Sara is seven now, Ivy four. My sister brings them out here a couple of times a year, and Dad and I go to Chicago alternate years for Christmas."

"Oh. That's nice."

"Which part?"

"All of it," she said honestly. Not being able

to see her mother and sister created a constant ache in her chest, made worse by Allie's illness. Neither of them had even seen Jacob. She didn't think he really understood the concept of grandmothers or aunts. Childbirth would have been so different if Mom and Allie both had been with her, had counted fingers and toes, held Jacob when he was tiny and bundled in a blanket so that only his head emerged.

"You miss your family," Seth said in a husky voice, even as he parked beside a farmhouse nestled in some big old trees. She'd given away more than she intended.

Finding out how much of a family man he was made her pray anew that he never learned she had it in her power to heal her sister, and hadn't done it.

A side door to the house opened, spilling light across the lawn. The man coming out was close to Seth's size with strong shoulders and a confident stride. His hair seemed to be white.

Seth opened his door and went to meet his father. They half hugged, in that guy way. Feeling shy, Robin got out, too.

Seth made quiet introductions before saying, "Let's get inside. Bed ready for Jacob?"

"Sure is. He doesn't need a crib?"

"No." For no good reason, she spoke barely above a whisper, as if there had to be listening ears out there. "At home, I have his mattress on the floor, but he'll be okay on a regular bed."

Michael Renner nodded. "What can I carry?"

As before, Seth carried Jacob inside and disappeared deeper into the house. Even a few days ago, she would have felt an anxious need to trot after him. It was too easy to trust this man.

"The bedroom is upstairs," his father said. "I already have gates out for the top and bottom of the stairs. Had 'em for my nieces, and held on to 'em in case my daughter had another one."

Robin let one of the duffels slide off her shoulder onto a stool drawn up to a breakfast bar on a big, granite-topped island. The kitchen was gorgeous, with Shaker-style maple cabinets, double ovens and a wrought-iron rack for pans hung over the stove top. The room was warm and welcoming, unlike Richard's kitchen.

"This is beautiful," Robin said, looking around. "Perfect."

His smile looked a lot like one of Seth's, except Michael's skin had more crinkles. He was still a good-looking man, and his hair wasn't white the way it had appeared outside but instead blond. Or, well, probably a mix. Seth had gotten his blue eyes from his father, but maybe his darker hair from his mother.

"I had it redone a few years ago." His tone was elaborately casual, but Robin suspected he knew to the day when the work had been done. He cleared his throat. "My wife—Seth's mother—had cancer. She'd dreamed of redoing the kitchen, and I wanted to make sure it happened." He looked around. "I just wish I'd gotten to it sooner."

Startled, Robin saw that she'd rested her hand on his forearm, and he was looking down at it. Embarrassed, she snatched back her hand.

He only smiled and said, "Thank you. Let me show you to your bedroom. I'm guessing you didn't get a lot of sleep earlier."

She wrinkled her nose. "I tried."

A low, rough chuckle charmed her.

"This is so nice of you," she hurried to say. "I mean, taking us in this way. Seth insisted you would before he'd even asked you. I guess you didn't have a lot of choice."

"Nonsense." His kindness was tangible. "Seth wouldn't have brought you here if you weren't in some serious trouble. I may be retired from the job, but I'm not incapable."

"Did Seth tell you about the man who tried to take my son?"

"He did."

"I've never been so scared in my life." And that included the two times she'd been certain Richard would kill her, when he'd lost even a semblance of restraint. "If anything happens, please save Jacob first. No matter what."

Eyes keen, he studied her face. Then he nodded.

At the same moment, she realized Seth was hovering in the kitchen doorway and had undoubtedly heard her request. Well, she would have asked the same of him when she got a chance, anyway. She tipped up her chin, saw his eyebrows twitch. Finally, he inclined his head in acknowledgment. And agreement, if she wasn't mistaken.

Then he came into the kitchen as if nothing had happened. "What do you need upstairs right now?"

Robin picked out the bag that held her toiletries and pajamas as well as clean clothes she could put on in the morning. Which was all of about two hours away, thanks to Jacob's early-rising habit.

Seth had wrapped Jacob in his blankie after lifting him out of the car, so she knew he had that. Blue bunny was...in that bag, she thought, along with a bunch of Jacob's clothes and toys. She picked it up, too, before being hit with an inexplicable feeling of abandonment.

"I suppose you're going home."

Seth shook his head. "No, I'll sack out here. Dad keeps my bedroom for me, except when my sister and her family are home and need it."

"Oh." Feeling uncharacteristically shy again, Robin said, "Well, good night, then."

"To you, too."

As usual, she hadn't a clue what he was thinking as he watched her follow his father toward the staircase.

HOLLOW-EYED FROM lack of sleep, pain throbbing in his temples, Seth poured himself his third cup of coffee for the morning and got on the phone as soon as he reached his desk.

It didn't take him long to connect with a sergeant at Seattle PD who proved willing to look for any domestic violence calls to Richard Winstead's address.

"Not a one," he said at last. "You know who Winstead is, don't you?"

"Better than you do, I suspect. I suppose the house is on a big piece of property."

"I'd call it an estate. Waterfront. That part of Magnolia—" He broke off. "You're suggesting neighbors wouldn't have been able to hear crashes or someone screaming."

"I'm asking."

"It's a butt-ugly house," the sergeant said thoughtfully. "I've heard it's like Bill Gates's, wired so lights turn on when someone walks into the room and off when they leave it. That kind of thing. Heat and appliances can be controlled from a distance by an app. I guess it was on the cover of a magazine for architects, but when I drove by I thought the really nice older brick mansions on each side were doing their best to lean away."

"I know the kind of place you mean," Seth said, kneading the back of his neck with the hand not holding the phone.

"I thought Winstead was divorced," Sergeant Hammond said thoughtfully.

"He is. Unless he's remarried, that I don't know about."

"Ah, let me check." The clatter of fingers on a keyboard came through the phone. "Nope." He paused. "The divorce wasn't contested. Is there something I should know about this?"

"His ex-wife is here in Lookout. I'm investigating the murder of a woman in the ex-wife's kitchen. Victim looked a lot like the ex. I think she was the intended victim."

"Robin Winstead."

"Robin Hollis now. She went back to her maiden name. And yes. She says Winstead swore if she ever tried to leave him, he'd kill her."

"You got any proof?"

"I'm working on it. Okay if I get back to you in a few days?"

"Looking forward to it."

Seth modified a template for requesting medical records and printed a couple of copies, then drove back to his father's house hoping Robin would be awake. She'd been deep under when he left, although Jacob was wide-awake and cheerful. Seth had disposed of the sodden diaper, cleaned up and dressed the little boy, and escorted him downstairs. He'd been happily settled in front of a short stack of pancakes when Seth left. Dad liked making pancakes.

Wan and sporting purple bruises beneath her eyes, Robin sat on one of the stools in the kitchen nursing a cup of coffee when he walked into the house.

He raised his eyebrows. "Where's Jacob?"

"Your dad took him outside. Apparently there's a tire swing out there?"

"Hey, yeah." His headache relented briefly. He half sat on the stool beside her, laying the manila folder on the granite surface of the island. "Ivy and Sara love it. Dad will watch out for him, don't worry."

Her freckles stood out more than usual, he saw, probably because the only other color in her face were those circles under her eyes. He wanted to smooth some of that stress away, massage her neck and shoulders until she moaned.

Instead, he kept his hands to himself as she smiled, looking as exhausted as he felt.

"I know. Your father's being really sweet. You, too. Jacob said you gave him another bath."

"We boys have to stick together." Man, he needed to get out of here. Seth flipped open the file and took a pen from his shirt pocket. "I need your signature."

She stared blankly at the permission form. Eventually, he thought she actually started taking it in, finally signing both copies and pushing them back to him. He gently removed the pen from her hand.

"Take a nap when Jacob does this afternoon, Robin. I'll bet you didn't get three hours of sleep last night."

She searched his face. "You look tired, too."

"I'll cut the day short if I can," he said gruffly. There was plenty he wanted to say and do, but he restrained himself, leaving with her a distantly polite "Thank you," grating as though he'd lost a layer of skin.

Chapter Nine

The next day, Robin came to the conclusion that Seth intended to stay at his father's house as long as she and Jacob were there.

His presence both relieved and unsettled her. Robin would have felt horribly guilty if his poor father had been left alone to deal with the awkwardness and extra work of guests he hadn't even invited. But when Seth was home, she became self-conscious, aware every second of where he was, whether he was watching her or they might touch in passing, how she looked…and of all the darkness in her past that he didn't know about.

When he came in the door on Tuesday, his expression was grim enough to alarm her. His face was harder than usual, the angles sharper.

To give herself a minute, she turned on the burner beneath the water that needed to boil for the pasta. "Something's wrong."

He shook his head, but the deeper lines

in his forehead and beside his mouth didn't smooth out. "Smells good."

She was making spaghetti, which Michael said was a favorite of his and was also a meal a two-year-old would eat. Robin asked fiercely, "Then why do you look like that?"

"Look like—" He scrubbed a hand over his face without having any effect, then glanced around. "Where's Dad?"

She grimaced. "Where do you think? He created a fiend when he put Jacob on that swing."

A faint smile rewarded her. It vanished almost immediately. "I got some of your medical records today."

"Oh." She couldn't meet his eyes.

"Several of the hospitals emailed records and X-rays. They were hard to look at."

"Surely you've handled domestic abuse cases before."

"I have. But damn, Robin. I didn't know any of the women as well as I do you. I didn't—" Seth shook off whatever he'd been about to say. "There were a couple of notes expressing doubt at how you were injured. I'm having trouble understanding why the doctors who saw you didn't call the police."

She clasped her hands together so he wouldn't see the tremor. "Richard, that's why.

He'd probably met most of the doctors at fund-raising events. He's that well-known. Slick, too. Along with always having a believable explanation, he was really good at seeming scared for me, loving. Looking back, I don't understand why I didn't speak up. Maybe I thought—"

Seth cut her off. "It's not on you, Robin. Abused women rarely ask for help in that situation. You have to know that. Maybe you didn't think you'd be believed, and you knew what the consequences would be once he got you home. Maybe you still loved him, had hope he really was sorry."

"No. Not that." She was glad of an excuse to turn away from his troubled gaze to stir the sauce and dump the spaghetti into the now-boiling water. "I was afraid of him. And yes, he's a lot more compelling than I am. I *didn't* think anybody would believe me."

"Even your family?"

"If Dad had still been alive, I would have gone to them." She thought. "But if I'd put Mom and Allie in the position of having to defend me, I don't know what Richard would have done. He had a temper, but mostly he was so cold." Hard not to shudder. "He could be smiling one second, knocking me to the floor the next. No warning. I didn't want him even remembering I *had* family."

Seth swore again. "How are you talking about this so calmly? Working on dinner as if it all happened to someone else?"

She huffed in disbelief. "You think I'm *calm*? I'm refusing to crumple up in a sobbing heap, that's all. Your people-reading skills need some fine-tuning."

He moved so fast, she didn't have a chance to retreat. He was suddenly right there in front of her, inches away, his fingers flexing as if he wanted to reach for her. His visible regret, even anguish, brought a lump to her throat. "I'm sorry," he said roughly. "I know better."

"No." Damn it, her eyes stung. Refusing to let herself cry, she took an angry swipe at her cheeks with the back of her hand. "Oh, crud. I'm a mess."

"Robin." Now his hands did close on her shoulders. "I swore I wouldn't do this, but I think I need…" He didn't have to finish the sentence. His hard embrace said it all.

She responded the way she had last time, taking comfort from him she didn't deserve but couldn't resist. Laying her cheek against his shoulder, she wrapped her arms around him and let herself lean against that solid body and soak in his strength. It could be for only a moment; she didn't want his father to walk in on them, and she couldn't let herself weaken for too long.

His heart vibrated against her breast, and she felt him rub his cheek against her hair. Or had he kissed her on the head? That lump in her throat had swelled to monumental proportions.

"Robin," he murmured. "You really get to me. You know that, don't you?"

She straightened enough to be able to see his face, eyes that had never been so blue. "Because you feel sorry for me?"

"Angry for you," he corrected. "You're a strong woman." His jaw flexed. "A beautiful woman. And I shouldn't have even said that."

"Why not?"

"As much as I want to kiss you, I need you to be able to trust me more." He made a sound in his throat. "Which means I should get my hands off you."

His arms tightened instead, for only an instant. Feeling his arousal, heat settled low in her belly.

"I like your hands on me," she admitted.

He groaned. "I'm trying to behave myself."

She ached to feel his mouth on hers, but how could she initiate anything when she still had secrets? Still, she gripped his shirt in both hands, unable to look away from him.

His head bent slowly, so slowly she knew he was giving her time to retreat. Instead, she pushed herself up on tiptoe to meet him.

APPARENTLY HIS RESOLVE was tissue thin, because Seth did exactly what he'd sworn he wouldn't: he kissed the woman who depended on him to protect her son and keep her safe.

The woman who'd drawn him since first sight.

He might want to devour her, but he did keep enough of a grip on himself to make the first contact gentle. A brush of his lips over hers. Back again. He lifted his head and saw the stunned pleasure on her face, her eyes melting caramel, her lips parted. That's all it took for him to lose it. He groaned, cradled the back of her head so he could angle it for the best fit, and deepened the kiss. His awareness of his surroundings blurred. All he knew was her, the soft press of her breasts against his chest, the taut arch of her back, her taste and breath and small, involuntary sounds. He gripped her butt to lift her, and somehow pulled out the elastic in her hair to free the silky mass to fall over his hand and her shoulders. He turned her, wanting to boost her onto the counter so he could get between her legs.

But…damn, there was a voice. Not *a* voice—his father's. And it was close.

"Shoot," he growled, bumping his forehead against hers. "Dad's coming."

With a gasp, Robin tore herself away. "Jacob!"

Her son. A boy who'd probably never seen his mommy being kissed by a man before. Even as Seth understood her alarm, he didn't like her obvious shock. She'd kissed him as much as he'd kissed her.

Her back to him, she mumbled, "I almost forgot the vegetable."

"Okay by me." He might have tried for lightness, but that came out husky. And, *hell*, he couldn't let his father see him like this.

Robin had found a chiding expression for him by the time Dad and Jacob came in the door from outside. Seth had almost hustled out of the kitchen when Jacob rushed to her.

"Mommy! I swinged *high*!"

She laughed and scooped him up for a hug. "I'll bet you did."

Seth kept going. "Gotta wash up."

He used the hall bathroom to wash his hands and wait for his body to accept defeat. Nothing more was going to happen tonight.

With the door open, he heard his father say, "Smells good."

"Like father, like son."

God, he loved even her voice, irresistibly warm.

This wasn't helping. Seth reached over to close the bathroom door and stared at himself in the mirror. Mostly, he saw the same bony face as always. He ran a hand over his jaw. Yeah, he could use a shave. And maybe his lips were a little swollen. He'd never seen himself as a handsome man, not like—

Disgusted with himself, he splashed some cold water on his face. Looks didn't make the man. And she'd welcomed his kiss, which he hoped wasn't a mistake.

When he returned to the kitchen, Jacob rushed to Seth, who hoisted him high over his head. The boy squealed in excitement and laughed. Seth lowered him to his feet and said, "I think it's time for dinner, buddy. What do you say we set you up at the table?"

"Thank you," Robin said distractedly.

He had to wonder whether her cheeks were pink from the heat of the stove or self-consciousness with him.

"Michael," she said, "will you get the garlic bread out of the oven?"

The house had a rarely used formal dining room. The family had always gathered in the kitchen, where the table easily seated six. Like the stair gates, Michael had kept a high chair, which Seth now strapped Jacob into. The kid immediately grabbed his spoon and began banging it on the tray. He chanted, "Sghetti! Sghetti! Sghetti!" until Michael distracted him with a piece of bread.

Seth caught an odd, possibly wistful expression from Robin, who'd paused to watch her son. He strolled over to her and, in a low voice, asked, "What are you thinking?"

"What? Oh! Just about dinner."

"Not just about dinner."

He thought she was concentrating on draining the spaghetti, but she said suddenly, although also quietly, "Just how much Jacob is enjoying attention from you and your dad. He's never really known a man very well. When his day-care operator's husband comes home, Jacob is really shy with him."

She poured the spaghetti into a large ceramic bowl and handed it to him. "Sauce is already on the table. I'll get the peas..." She glanced around, as if sure she'd forgotten something.

"Parmesan?" he suggested.

A minute later, they sat down around the table. Seth thought of how empty his own house was, and didn't like knowing that Robin and Jacob wouldn't stay forever. In fact…was that what she'd been worrying about, too?

His father and he had been giving Jacob something important. Clearly, Robin didn't have any men in her life to replace them. Seth switched his gaze to the boy, who had cheerfully splattered his cheeks in red sauce as he switched between a fork and his hands to shovel in the pasta.

"Sghet-ti," he sang around a bite.

Seth laughed. "Let me wipe your face."

Jacob submitted to the cleaning, then grinned at Seth and deliberately smeared his hands over his face.

Laughing again, Seth said, "Okay, we'll wait to clean you up until you're done eating."

"This is an especially perilous meal," Robin said with amusement. "You notice I used a *giant* bib."

"I did. Although I think he's got some sauce on his sleeves."

She rolled her eyes humorously. He liked that she didn't stress over messes.

Aware his father's gaze rested on him, Seth concentrated for a minute on eating. What he'd just discovered was that he didn't want any other man in Robin's life, or to fill Jacob's need for a father.

The realization felt like a tiny lurch in the fabric of reality. Man, he was getting *way* ahead of himself. Yes, he knew now that she hadn't exaggerated her abuse at the hands of Richard Winstead. At least that much she'd told him was the truth. He remained uneasy, in part because she must have known that she could have gone to the cops in Seattle. Whatever Winstead's reputation, her medical records were overwhelmingly persuasive, and Seth hadn't yet received them all.

Was Robin truly still so terrified of the man, she wore blinders, thinking she had to live her entire life on the run? Or was there more?

As IF SHE were a child again, Robin wound the tire swing around and around before she climbed into it. Spinning until she couldn't tell up from down was fun then. So why wouldn't it be now?

Because she already knew how it felt to have her life spin out of control?

To heck with it. She was going to do this.

She put one leg at a time through the tire, worn bald before it found a new life. Firmly gripping the rope right above the knot, Robin took a deep breath and lifted her foot from the ground.

The tire spun once, twice, three times, gaining speed. She leaned back and looked up at the tree branches and the sky. Her eyes couldn't focus anymore, so fast did everything tear by. Oh, Lord—bile rose into her throat. She was going to be sick. She had to stop… With a bounce and a countertwirl, the tire slowed and she hung there for an endless moment.

"Fun?" Seth asked.

She clapped her hand over her mouth and squirmed out of the tire, falling to her knees on the grass. She was humiliatingly aware that he'd crouched beside her and was gently rubbing her back while she dry-heaved.

Thank God, she didn't quite puke, but her mouth tasted awful and she felt as if she was still in motion.

With a hint of humor, he said, "You wouldn't catch me dead doing that anymore."

"Ugh." Robin let her head sag. "It used to be fun."

"Stinks to get older."

Her stomach muscles hurt and her head still swam. "Just what I needed to hear."

He chuckled. "Lie down. You'll feel better."

Since she wasn't capable of doing much else, she sprawled onto the grass on her back, arms and legs splayed. There were the tree branches above her again, still moving—no, only the leaves danced in a breeze—against the blue backdrop. Seth had risen effortlessly to his feet and looked down at her. At the moment, he was the quintessential detective, wearing dark slacks, a white button-down shirt, a badge clipped to his thin black belt and a big black gun holstered at his hip.

"Why are you home?" she asked.

"Decided to take the afternoon off. Hey, let me get you something to drink." He disappeared from her limited range of vision.

Something to drink? To rinse her mouth out, he meant. Robin ran her tongue over her teeth and made a horrible face. He was right, though; she did feel better with her body, head to heels, in contact with the nice, solid earth.

Seth walked into sight with a can of lemon-lime soda in his hand. Her gaze zeroed in on it.

He laughed, crouched again and helped her sit up, then popped the top off the can and handed it to her. Then he sat, too, his back to the thick bole of the maple tree.

Robin sipped cautiously at the drink.

"I've been thinking," he said in a casual tone that instantly made her wary. "Why don't you use my phone and call your mom and sister? It should be safe." He shifted his weight to dig his smartphone out of a pocket.

She gave her head a hard, almost frantic shake. Not the reaction he'd expected, she saw from his narrowed eyes.

Or maybe it was. Was he just being nice to suggest she call home, or did he have another motive? Could his phone be set up to record everything she said?

Sure it could, although she felt guilty. If he was just being nice...

"Why not?" he said softly.

And she knew. This was a setup.

"All I'd do is scare them if I told them what's been happening. I'll wait until, well, things are resolved." Like Richard behind bars? Uh-huh, and how long would he stay there? He'd have no problem paying bail, or hiring the sharpest, most amoral attorney in Portland or Seattle to represent him.

If she stayed in hiding, how would Richard ever be caught doing anything to *get* arrested? Did Seth, a small-town detective, have a chance in hell of finding proof Richard had hired the unknown stranger who had tried to steal Jacob?

Of course not.

Sitting cross-legged, she asked somberly, "What are we doing here, Seth? Jacob and I can't become the guests who never go away. Your father doesn't deserve that. It's not that I'm eager to go home—" would the rental even feel like home? "—but if I don't become bait, there's no way to nail Richard. And how's that going to work, when I refuse to put Jacob at risk?"

"I wouldn't ask you—" He sounded offended.

"Then what?" Robin jumped to her feet. "You should have let me go." She left him and hurried toward the house.

The tension was getting to her. That was the only explanation. It was ironic, since she was certain she hadn't been safer in years. Here she was with a police detective and a retired cop guarding her and her child.

If only Seth didn't inspire feelings in her she'd believed to be dead. After that last year with Richard, how could she have melted in Seth's arms the way she had? If they'd really been alone, she doubted she'd have stopped him if he had hauled her off to his bedroom.

So, okay, he was attracted to her, but even assuming there actually was a resolution—whatever that might be—and she stayed in Lookout instead of returning to Seattle, why would he go for a woman with such a turbulent background, a woman who was also an emotional disaster? Tall, athletic, sexy and with those startlingly blue eyes, he surely had women coming onto him wherever he went.

And all that was assuming she didn't end up back in Seattle not by choice, but because she had to fight a murder charge.

Face it, she shouldn't be thinking about a man at all, when she ought to be praying she could go home to Seattle so that she could give Allie one of her kidneys.

Looking through the window over the sink, she saw Seth walking slowly toward the house, lines of perturbation showing on his forehead, his gaze somehow turned inward.

Sure, she thought desperately. Just put him out of her head. Nothing to it.

If only he wasn't so ever-present…and so sexy.

Chapter Ten

Seth was already getting to know Sergeant Gordon Hammond of the Seattle PD well enough to be comfortable talking out possible strategies. Robin was right; they'd never catch this SOB red-handed unless they opened an apparent window to tempt him into making a move.

With her permission, this morning Seth had forwarded her medical records to Hammond, who'd sounded as grim as Seth felt when they talked this morning.

Hammond had been finding it harder than he'd expected to keep an eye on Richard Winstead's whereabouts.

"He has a private plane, I've learned. If we had a warrant, I could be informed when or if he flies in and out of Boeing Field, but as it is, I don't have a good contact there. Some of his activities are well-publicized, but there are enough gaps, I'd have to have someone on him twenty-four seven to keep track of his whereabouts."

"What about this week?"

"Well, in theory the man works full-time. He's a partner in a major law firm, after all. In practice, he attends every city council meeting, and he's on at least two subcommittees. In the next couple of weeks, all those meetings are during the day."

"Committees?"

"Housing, Health, Energy and Workers' Rights is one, and isn't that a mishmash, and then there's Governance, Equity and Technology." Hammond was clearly reading off a website or his notes. "Both committees can meet up to a couple of times a week."

"A man of dependable judgment," Seth said drily.

The sergeant snorted. "I suppose his civic activism is good for the law firm."

"Oh, I imagine his partners consider it part of his contribution to the firm's profits."

More thoughtfully, Hammond said, "I'm assuming there'd be some record if he *didn't* attend a meeting he was supposed to be at."

"I'd rather know in advance when he's out of town." Seth rested his elbows on his desk. "And then there's the problem of his hired help."

"Since you can't be sure Winstead has ever

been in Lookout, that's the bigger problem, I'd say."

"Ms. Hollis hinted at the possibility of offering herself as bait. I don't like it, but I might find a way to make it appear she's back home at the rental." His department didn't have any female officers, but the county and a neighboring town or two did. He might be able to borrow a stand-in.

He frowned. What were the odds he'd find one who bore any resemblance to the woman who was currently giving him sleepless nights?

"If she's willing to testify," the sergeant said hesitantly, "we could bring him up on the abuse."

"Even if he were convicted, he'd be out of jail in the blink of an eye and mad as hell."

"How did he find her? Twice?"

Seth pinched the bridge of his nose between his thumb and forefinger. "It's harder to disappear than it used to be. We both know that. Doesn't sound like she had any professional help, either."

"And he can afford to write a blank check to a PI."

Seth gritted his teeth. "If I can find out who that is, I'd like to have some words with him."

Hammond agreed, and promised to let Seth

know what he learned about Winstead's plans in advance.

A report half an hour later that shots had been fired at the high school pulled Seth away from his desk. Over the next hours, he interviewed dozens of students and the baseball coaching staff before finally arresting a young idiot who appeared shocked at the official response and insisted, "If I'd really wanted to shoot someone, I would have! All I did was…"

Get himself in some serious trouble. But at least there were no victims. Thank God.

Of course, writing reports killed the rest of Seth's working day. He didn't know when he'd been so glad to leave work. If that's what he was actually doing, he mused. Cops had been known to blur the relationship line between professional and personal, but not him. With Robin and Jacob, though, he'd crossed right on over. In fact, he wasn't sure he could find the line again, unless and until they walked out of his life.

Halfway to his father's house, Seth was still brooding. That was also the moment when he realized he hadn't been paying any attention to the traffic around him. Usually it was instinct. Given that he could lead someone right to Robin and Jacob, he'd been even more careful than usual in the past few days.

A silver sedan and a black crossover were behind him. He took an abrupt turn at the next intersection. The crossover kept going, the sedan stuck behind him. Both roads were well-used, so that didn't necessarily mean anything. Two more turns, and he'd lost the sedan, too. Still, he zigzagged the rest of the way to his father's, and remained uneasy when he got there, watching for any traffic passing on the quiet country road at the foot of the driveway.

He went in and said hello to everyone, changed into old clothes he kept here for the times he helped his father with yard work or maintenance and went back out. He knew where to find the crawler for sliding under cars, and used it and a flashlight to examine the underside of his Ford F-150 pickup truck. He slid his fingers inside the bumper and beneath the license plates, failing to find anything.

When he sat up, his father and Robin both stood over him.

"Car problem?" his father asked.

"Where's Jacob?" He turned his head.

"Watching TV."

"Nothing wrong with the truck. I just got to thinking how easy it would be to plant a tracker."

It was Robin he looked at when he said, "I'd be bound to lead someone to you eventually."

"What a wonderful thought." She whirled and hurried back into the house.

His father nodded at his pickup. "You sure you would have found it?"

"Not a hundred percent, no. I need to take a look inside, too, even though I kept the doors locked."

Michael shrugged. They both knew how easy it was to pop a window and unlock a car or truck. Patrol officers carried a tool to help them do exactly that for citizens who'd locked their keys inside their own cars. Seth, for one, could do it in twenty seconds or less.

"Robin cooking again?"

His father scowled. "I offered to grill, but she insisted. Seems to think she owes me something for letting her and the boy stay here. As if they're any kind of burden."

Seth grinned. "When the truth is, you're enjoying the company."

"Nice lady who cooks, great kid. Of course I am." His father smiled. "Remember how whiny Ivy was? And that stretch when I swear the only word Sara knew was *no*?"

Laughing now, Seth said, "Yeah, I think that's why Grace brought the girls out here that time. She was ready to tear her hair out. Huh. Jacob is bound to learn the power of 'no.'"

They were both chuckling when they returned to the house, where spaghetti was once again on the menu.

Robin apologized. "I made way too much sauce. I don't know what I was thinking. Usually at home I freeze it in small batches, and I could have done that, but I thought why not have it another night?"

"Sghetti," her son said happily.

Jacob was less enthusiastic about the broccoli until Seth held up a clump and said, "Look, a tree," and gobbled it like a monster. Jacob gleefully followed suit.

Robin shook her head. "Why didn't I ever think of that?"

They all laughed.

His dad said, "So what's this I heard about a shooting today?"

Robin's alarmed gaze swung to him.

"A stupid teenager, what else? He was mad because the baseball coach suspended him after he was arrested at a kegger. He just wanted to scare him a little in payback. Apparently the kid hunts, and insists he made sure he didn't hurt anybody."

"I hope he wasn't eighteen," Michael said.

"Had his birthday in January. Boy's in trouble. I don't think he gets it."

Seth saw Robin eyeing Jacob with some wariness, clearly concerned for him.

His father declared that he'd take KP duty tonight, and Seth sat Robin down to talk. They went outside onto the deck so Jacob could run around on the lawn and she could keep an eye on him.

"Do you know whether Richard kept an investigator on retainer?" Seth asked.

"Like a firm, you mean? Why would he?" She made a face. "Before he set out to find me, I mean."

"He may have other ongoing problems. You can't be the only person who has seen behind his facade."

She seemed to be thinking about that, but shook her head in the end. "I don't know about that. Anyway, wouldn't his law firm employ investigators?"

Not ones Winstead would dare use for sleazy work. "Did he ever receive threats?" Seth asked.

"Not that I know of, although he did—"

She covered the alarm quickly enough to make Seth doubt what he'd seen. "Did what?" he prodded.

"Well, I was going to say that the house is

well-staffed. That would provide protection when he was home."

"It might. Did he drive himself, or have a driver?"

"Sometimes he'd have someone drive him," she said slowly. "Mostly not."

Seth made a mental note to have Hammond look into Winstead's employees.

"Did he have any employees you'd classify as bodyguards?"

Robin jumped to her feet. "Jacob?"

Seth had been keeping an eye on the kid, too, and had seen him go behind the big cedar tree. Before he could tell her, the boy peeked around the trunk. "I hid," he told her proudly.

"No more hiding," she said firmly. "Stay where I can see you."

Seth said, "Hey, I saw a soccer ball in the garage. Let me go get it."

Once he brought it out, he spent a few minutes showing Jacob how to kick the ball and move with it. It was a kid-size one, another leftover from his nieces' visits.

Shaking his head as he returned to the deck, Seth said, "I think it'll be a few years before he's ready to join a team."

"His coordination isn't quite there, is it?"

"Nope." Where had they left off? "Body-guard," he said, remembering.

"Yes, he did," she said, sounding composed. "The man was his occasional driver. I wondered, though, because he looked like a bodybuilder, you know?"

"What was his name?"

"Oh, boy. I didn't see much of him. McCoy? McCormack? Mc-something. He was there only about the last year of our marriage. He probably got axed after I made my getaway."

There was something a little too casual about her speech. Seth studied her. "You think his real role was prison guard?"

"Probably. It seemed like every time I went outside, he was *there*. Stepping out of the garage or whatever, eyes on me. You know Richard wouldn't have tolerated incompetence."

"No, I don't suppose he would have," Seth said thoughtfully. He couldn't guess what she wasn't telling him, but he'd lay money there was something. Had she had a relationship with the man? Had he helped her, or at least turned a blind eye, when she escaped? No, if that were the case, why wouldn't Robin say?

This was only one reason why he should have kept his hands off her.

"Could this guy have been the one who grabbed Jacob?"

"No." Not so coincidentally, she chose then to turn her head and focus on Jacob, who had given up on the soccer ball and was rolling down a slight incline.

"You sound sure."

"The guy in the mask wasn't bulky enough."

"But he was too big to be Richard."

"There's...a lot of ground in between, you know."

"Like me, say."

She stole a look at him, her gaze sliding from his shoulders down his torso and along his outstretched legs. Flushing, she said, "You're at least as tall as the bodyguard. You're just not...not muscle-bound."

He had to shift his weight to accommodate his body's response to her lingering inspection, and the betraying warmth in her cheeks. The temptation was there to tease, but Seth hadn't forgotten his earlier thought. *Stick to business.*

"Does your mother know you found a body in your house?"

"No!" She stared at him in outrage. "I told you!"

"You said you didn't want to call now. You might have let her know when it first happened. Say, when you were staying at the inn."

"Well, I didn't."

HE STILL THOUGHT she was lying to him, and he was right. Robin knew she'd never been a very good liar, which was an irony for someone who'd spent two and a half years lying about something as basic as her name.

Even when she wasn't looking at him, his sharp, assessing gaze made her want to squirm...and tell him everything. She had to get away.

Acid burning her stomach, she asked, "Are we done?"

"We can be." Seth raised his eyebrows. "Doesn't mean we have to rush inside."

"I'm lucky Jacob has entertained himself this long."

"You're right. I'm on the job."

With easy athleticism, he bounced to his feet. In no time he had a giggling Jacob chasing him around the yard. When he let himself be caught, Seth turned the tables and lumbered after her son. He scooped up Jacob, powerful biceps flexing, tucked him under one arm like a football and raced around the yard.

Breath catching, Robin started to rise to her feet. Jacob would be scared... But he wasn't, she saw in astonishment. They both ended up sprawled on the grass, laughing.

She'd swear Seth was enjoying himself as

much as Jacob was. In that moment, she felt something entirely unfamiliar. *Yearning* was the word she came up with. Why couldn't Jacob have a father like this, instead of the one she prayed he never meet? What couldn't *she* have a man like this?

Seth embodied such contradictions: ruthlessness and a capacity for protection, with kindness and a powerful defensive instinct. The guardedness that she guessed was typical of cops with an ability to live in the moment with a little boy.

He did want her, but Robin couldn't imagine he wouldn't despise her once he knew she'd been tested three years ago and been found a match to give her sister a kidney, but hadn't done it. Endless rounds of dialysis kept Allie from having any kind of a life. She couldn't hold a job or even live alone. If she had a boyfriend, she'd never said so during any of her brief conversations with Robin. Allie must hate her, Robin thought with familiar self-loathing. When she screwed up her life, she'd damaged Mom's and Allie's lives plenty, too.

Maybe she should give up and tell Seth everything. Get it over with. Why put off the inevitable?

Because he was a cop. He couldn't let her

confession that she'd killed a man slide. She could claim self-defense, but since she'd been trespassing at the time, Robin suspected law enforcement wouldn't see it that way.

She discovered suddenly that he'd gone completely still, and she was the object of his unnervingly intent gaze. For charged seconds, Robin couldn't look away. If he could see right through her…well, let him.

In the end, she took the coward's way out and fled into the house.

SETH MADE SOME calls to neighboring jurisdictions on Friday, and determined that Hood River County Sheriff's Department employed a female deputy who might pass as Robin to a distant watcher who saw her moving past a lighted window in the house. She wouldn't fool anyone who got a good look at her, though.

There was a lot Seth didn't like about the idea of setting a trap, however. Starting with the possibility that if Winstead was as good a shot as Robin thought, he could fire from across the street, put a bullet through Deputy Jennifer Hadleigh's head and vanish in seconds. Of course, he'd discover in no time that he'd killed the wrong woman—again—and they'd be back where they started.

Since Seth hadn't worked with the deputy,

he had no idea how competent she was, either. Or whether she'd agree to this scheme.

What he did know was that Robin would balk if he suggested putting another woman at risk in her place. That needn't stop them, of course, but while he wouldn't describe himself as sensitive, he knew what Robin desperately needed was to feel in control of her life, not in even less control.

Sometimes, how you made something happen was as important as the result.

The wistful, maybe sad expression on her face when she watched him play with Jacob out on the lawn kept coming back to him. Ignoring his father's curiosity, Seth had followed her last night after she announced her intention of going to bed at a ridiculously early hour. With a hand on her arm, he'd stopped her at the foot of the stairs.

"You don't have to run away from me," he'd said in a low voice.

She'd huffed out a breath. "I have no idea what you're talking about. I'm tired. Jacob's an early riser."

"You have no idea how much I want to barrel right through the walls you've built to keep everyone out."

Her breath hitched. "Please don't," she'd

said so softly he'd had to lean forward to hear her. "I need them."

And then she'd jerked away and dashed upstairs, never glancing back.

He'd had to go back to the living room and face his father, who knew him well enough to have a good idea how mixed up he was where Robin was concerned. Fortunately, Dad was also smart enough not to push too hard.

Forcing himself to concentrate on work, Seth sent an email request to Sergeant Hammond inquiring about Winstead's current and former employees. After that, he turned his attention to other investigations that had gone on the back burner. The most significant was a recent series of burglaries, car prowls and mail theft. He'd begun to wonder if they were all being committed by the same person or persons.

He'd started his career with Portland Police Bureau until his mother got sick and he took the job here in town so he could count on being free to help both his parents. Once Mom was gone and his father was past the worst of his grief, Seth could have gone back to the much larger law-enforcement agency, but had discovered by then that he liked the pace of small-town policing and the independence of being the only detective on the Lookout police force. Four years later, he didn't have any regrets.

The kind of crime spree occurring here now was far more common in a city. While patrolling as a rookie, he'd broken up a ring of thieves by sheer luck. Turning a corner in a residential neighborhood, he saw a man leave a panel truck in a driveway, scan for anyone watching and stroll around the side of the house. Seth had parked where his marked unit would be hidden behind the larger panel truck and waited. He hadn't been surprised when the guy reappeared with his arms full. When he saw Seth, he leaped into the truck and tried to take off. Seth had taken the precaution of blocking the tires.

Turned out the electronics and jewelry he'd just stolen was nothing compared to what was already in the back of the truck. Once a responding detective identified the guy, they found his garage full of stolen household goods. Fingerprints nailed two of his friends, who were holding more stolen goods. A lot of people were really happy to come into the police station to identify their stolen items.

Seth had already talked to the patrol officers here in Lookout as well as the county patrol sergeant, and urged everyone to keep an eye out for something as simple as a car moving from one mailbox to another—particularly if the driver was removing mail from the boxes rather than tossing fliers in newspaper boxes, say.

Sooner or later, a sharp-eyed cop would be in the right place at the right time.

Listening with half an ear to the police radio, he checked email. Oh, good—a response from Hammond already.

HEARING THE TV, Robin stepped into the living room. There was a lot of laughter from a talk show that didn't look like anything she could imagine interesting Michael. But gosh, who knew? He was in his recliner with his feet up, apparently watching. Maybe he usually spent all day glued to the television. Maybe he loved soap operas and out of self-consciousness had been depriving himself. It was none of her business.

But seemingly still unaware of her scrutiny, he grabbed the remote and irritably flicked through several stations.

"Hi," she said. "Sorry to interrupt. I'm making soup and sandwiches for Jacob and me, and I thought I'd see if you're ready for lunch."

"You don't have to wait on me." The TV went dark, and he dropped the remote onto the end table. After a minute he said, "I'm fighting some heartburn, but maybe eating something mild will help."

"Are you sure it's heartburn? It might be worth getting checked out at a walk-in clinic."

He smiled at her and lowered the footrest. "I've seen my doctor, and I'm on prescription meds for this. It comes and goes."

"Is my cooking too spicy? I could—"

Michael looked and sounded a lot like his son when he laughed. "It's probably that damn beef jerky I decided to gnaw on earlier."

She laughed. "That does sound like a good possibility. Well, lunch will be ready in ten minutes."

In the kitchen, she heated soup and grilled cheese sandwiches. Which might be a little fatty for someone suffering from heartburn, but Michael could decide that for himself.

Jacob, who'd been playing with his blocks, decided he needed to use the bathroom. She was leading him down the hall when she heard a rattling sound from behind her. The back door handle turning? Had Seth come home early again for some reason?

She glanced back to see the reappearance of a nightmare.

A masked man just outside lifted a gun to slam the butt into the glass pane in the door. Glass shattered, and he reached inside for the lock.

Robin screamed.

Chapter Eleven

Scream still ringing in her ears, she backed out of sight. Michael was at her side instantly. To her shock, he held a big handgun that he must have been carrying all along without her noticing.

"Get Jacob upstairs," he ordered her in a low voice. "Find something to defend yourself with if you can. Don't argue. Now *run*."

She lifted Jacob into her arms, bent over to make a smaller target and ran.

The intruder had started across the kitchen. "Stop!" he yelled.

But she was out of sight, leaping up the stairs. Terrified for Michael down below, but Jacob had to come first.

A bullet smacked into the wallboard just behind her. Three more steps, two. Panting, she debated. Which room? Which room?

Another bark of a gun firing, then a second shot. *Please, God, don't let Michael be killed.*

She lunged into the bathroom, shoved the door shut with her hip and set Jacob down in the cast-iron tub. "Lie down, honey. Don't get up until I tell you to." After whirling back to lock the door, she saw Jacob struggling to stand. "Down! Do you hear me?" She'd never spoken to him so sharply before. She couldn't let herself care that tears ran down his cheeks.

Shouts. More gunshots.

"Mommy?" he whispered but curled up in a ball in the tub.

"Don't move," she snapped. Weapon. Had to find a weapon.

She yanked open the medicine cabinet, but it was nearly empty. She'd brought shampoo and gel in here, but no hairspray. Roll-on deodorant wouldn't hurt a flea.

Her eye fell on the toilet, and she snatched up the porcelain lid. Then she positioned herself by the door, listening hard. A couple of the stairs squeaked, this being an old house. She'd hear anyone coming.

Unless he'd already gunned down Michael and taken the stairs while she was talking to Jacob.

More scared than she'd been even during the earlier abduction attempt, Robin held her breath and waited.

SETH WAS WADDING up the wrappings from the sandwich he'd just finished when his radio crackled.

The dispatcher sounded typically calm as she gave the code for shots fired. "The caller can't see the gunman but thinks he or she must be on the neighbor's property. Any available units respond."

The address was Dad's.

Feeling as if he'd just been gut-punched, Seth accelerated from the curb, lights already flashing. He reported his current location and intention of responding with ETA. Two other officers chimed in, as did one county deputy who seemed to be the nearest of all of them. Then Seth hit the siren, too, and wove his way through the streets toward his father's house.

He decided not to call either his father or Robin, in case they were hiding. Seth reminded himself that Dad wouldn't be easy to take by surprise. He was carrying, and hadn't lost any of his reflexes or skills.

Dad would do anything to protect Robin and Jacob.

Five minutes.

If any of them died, if that bastard took Jacob… Seth's jaw ached and fear swelled in his chest.

The deputy reported on the radio that he

was turning into the driveway. He saw no vehicles, didn't hear gunshots.

Seth was close, flying down the narrow, two-lane country road. He got on the radio. "I'm two minutes out. Wait for backup."

The deputy agreed.

Seth took the turn into the driveway at high speed, leaving on his siren and lights as he bumped up the driveway.

He braked right beside the sheriff's department car. The deputy was crouched behind an open door. Didn't look young enough to be a rookie, thank God. Seth was glad to see he, too, wore a vest. After Seth had been shot while with Portland PB, he'd never slacked off wearing his on the job, uncomfortable as they sometimes were.

"This is my father's house," he explained. "There was an attempt to abduct a toddler in town a few days ago—"

"I heard about it."

"He and his mother are holed up here with Dad, who is a retired cop."

They agreed to split up, the deputy going to the front door, Seth slipping around to the side door. He held his Glock in a two-fisted grip, the barrel pointed down. The quiet didn't reassure him; Dad and Robin would have heard the sirens and come out.

Then he saw the door standing open, glass pane shattered, and he knew real terror.

ROBIN FINALLY REALIZED she was going to pass out if she didn't breathe. What was *happening*?

From the tub came quiet, hiccupping sobs, but Jacob stayed put.

Did she dare open the door and take a look out?

No. If it was safe, Michael would tell her. If he was dead…it wasn't safe.

Her hands shook. She rested the toilet lid on the vanity top but kept her grip on it.

She had to believe Richard wouldn't shoot through the door, risking the bullet hitting the son his ego demanded he claim. Because this was an old house, the bathroom door was a solid slab of wood, not flimsy like the one in her rental house.

Wait, she told herself. *Wait*.

If only she had her phone.

With no clock or watch, she couldn't see the minutes as they passed. Time felt compressed, or maybe stretched; either way, she had no sense of how long it had been since she heard anything but Jacob.

Except suddenly there were voices downstairs, loud commanding ones. Richard, insisting she come out and hand over Jacob? No, that was an exclamation of alarm. It couldn't be Seth, could it? How would he have known to come?

In the act of fumbling to undo the old-fashioned lock, her fingers froze. Michael wouldn't have had a chance to call 9-1-1 until after the shooting stopped. If he was alive.

No, she didn't dare assume this was a police response.

SETH SWORE VICIOUSLY at the sight of his father on the floor, leaning against the wall but listing to one side. His left hand was clamped to his bloody shoulder. His right hand held a gun that rested on his thighs. Blood matted his hair, and his eyes were glassy.

"Dad!" Seth crouched beside him and gently pried the weapon from his hand.

"I hit the bastard. He must have been wearing a vest."

"But you aren't." Should have provided one, he thought—except he'd convinced himself nobody would find Robin here.

"Robin and the boy, upstairs," his father grunted.

"Gunman?"

"Gone."

The deputy was suddenly there. "Ambulance is en route."

Seth swiveled on his heels. "Will you stay with him?"

"Yeah, let me grab something to stop the bleeding." He returned in seconds with a pile of kitchen towels.

Seth didn't holster his Glock as he moved silently up the stairs. If his father had hit his head, he could have briefly lost consciousness and not know it. If he had…

Seth called, "Robin?"

"Seth?"

Relief at hearing her voice poured through him. "Jacob with you?"

"He's… We were in the bathroom."

Once he reached the hall above and saw her waiting, he wanted desperately to take her in his arms. Instead, he ordered her to go back into the bathroom while he cleared this floor. That didn't take long. Through his own bedroom window, he saw the circus outside: four police vehicles all with flashing lights, and an ambulance coming up the driveway.

How had the intruder made his getaway? The roads had been empty for the past half a mile or more.

Once he had holstered his handgun and returned to the bathroom, he couldn't stop himself from gathering woman and boy into an embrace that was probably too tight.

ROBIN SAT IN a chair holding Jacob on her lap, and watched Seth pace the waiting room. He hadn't wanted to let her come to the hospital, but she'd pointed out that hiding was currently hopeless. Richard knew where she was.

Besides, if she and Jacob hadn't accompanied him, Seth would have had to post at least one officer to guard her at his father's house. That seemed wasteful.

Guilt balled in her stomach like a too-big serving of potato salad that had gone bad. Twice someone had offered to get her a soda, but Robin had shaken her head both times. She was already queasy.

She should never have let Seth take her and Jacob to his father's house. Now Michael was in surgery to have a bullet removed. He'd been shot because of her, just as it was her fault that a perfectly nice woman had been brutally murdered and her family left to grieve. She felt like a Jonah, endangering everyone around her. Sooner or later, Seth would notice that her life was a train wreck and get smart enough to jump out of the way.

On his circle around the room, he paused in front of her. "You okay?"

Robin nodded, even though she wasn't.

"Let me take him." Seth bent to reach for the small boy she held.

Sound asleep, Jacob became deadweight. Her arm had gone numb twenty minutes ago. Still, she made an automatic protest. "I'm fine."

"No, you're not," Seth growled, and pried the boy out of her arms. Jacob's eyelids didn't even flicker during the transfer. Holding Jacob snugly against one shoulder, Seth went back to pacing. The sight was incongruous given that he still wore a Kevlar vest and a handgun at his hip. A man simultaneously capable of violence and tenderness.

She had the sudden imagine of him walking the floor with his own child someday. No gun, pajama pants hanging low on lean hips, powerful torso bare as he comforted his baby by skin-to-skin contact. Patient, strong, affectionate.

Her distress rose like floodwaters behind a dike.

He'd be an amazing father.

Robin had to move. Rising stiffly to her feet, she said, "I need the restroom."

"I'll walk you."

"It's just around—"

The blue eyes skewered her. "You don't go anywhere without me. Remember?"

She nodded and let him usher her around the corner to an unoccupied restroom.

He opened the door and verified that it was empty before he let her go in.

She didn't dawdle the way she might have if he hadn't been hovering outside. Instead, they marched back to the waiting room.

Robin perched on the same chair she'd occupied before. "You still haven't heard from Sergeant Hammond?"

"It hasn't been that long."

It felt like forever. Her sense of passing time was definitely skewed today.

She wasn't certain that it was Richard who'd shot Michael, but she thought so. It was true she had barely caught a glimpse of the intruder, but mostly she was going on his voice. She *knew* his voice.

Seth hadn't argued. In fact, even before his father was put in the back of the ambulance, he'd called the Seattle PD sergeant, asking him to locate her ex-husband.

The surgeon walked into the small waiting room, his mask dangling around his neck. "Detective Renner?"

Robin was on her feet without conscious thought. Seth faced him.

He smiled. "Your father came through the surgery fine. We'll keep him overnight mostly because of the potential for concussion."

A bullet had grazed his head. Michael, of course, had said it wasn't more than a scratch.

"Good," Seth said hoarsely. "When can I see him?"

Probably another forty-five minutes. A nurse would come out to get him.

After the surgeon left as quickly as he'd appeared, Seth sank onto a chair. For once, his vulnerability showed. "*God.* To think Dad had to retire to get shot."

Robin's guilt increased. She made herself sit down, too, but felt her whole body vibrating. "You mean, he had to meet *me* to get shot!" she exclaimed.

Seth frowned at her. "He wanted to help."

"And look what happened," she challenged him. "Will you let me leave?"

"Hell, no!" he snapped, anger flaring. "Is that what you think? You're too much trouble?"

"I know I am!" Seeing Jacob squirm, she pressed her lips together.

Seth jiggled her son with easy competence until he settled back down in what was obviously a comfortable embrace. "No, Robin." His voice was a rumble, bass to Richard's tenor, suddenly soft with compassion in contrast to the frustration of a minute ago. "We'll find a way out for you, and we'll do it together."

Looking down at her clasped hands, she nodded because that's what he'd expect. He hadn't said where she and Jacob would go next, who else would be at risk to try to keep them safe. When she found out, then she'd have to make a decision.

Seth's phone vibrated on his hip. He picked it up, said, "It's Hammond," and answered with a terse, "Renner."

When she reached for Jacob, he let her take him.

MORE TO KEEP from waking Jacob than because he expected to say anything he didn't want Robin to hear, Seth walked out into the hall to take the call.

Hammond asked first about Michael.

"He's out of surgery, no permanent damage. No thanks to Winstead. Did you have any luck finding him?"

"No." The sergeant did not sound happy about it. "I'm getting the runaround from the law firm and his housekeeper. A senior partner claims Winstead is conducting confidential business this afternoon. Housekeeper says Mr. Winstead will be entertaining guests this evening for dinner. No, she didn't see him this morning, but she rarely does. He is an early riser and has usually eaten and left the house by the time she arrives."

"She doesn't live in."

"She says no one does. She did admit that there is an apartment over the garage, however, and another apartment in the house built for servant quarters. She just claims neither are currently occupied."

He'd ask Robin about that.

"Airplane is gone, no flight plan filed." Hammond paused. "Anything on your end?"

"An officer called rental car companies. Richard Winstead hasn't popped up anywhere."

"So he either borrowed a car or has ID in an alternate name."

"I'd guess the second. He wouldn't want to trust even a friend to keep his mouth shut."

"No." Hammond sighed. "I have a patrol officer down at Boeing Field. I can't guarantee he won't get called away, though."

"Understood."

"Your father doesn't think he wounded the guy?"

"Dad says he went for chest shots. One knocked the intruder backward into the kitchen island, but he rebounded quickly, fired a couple more shots and fled. Had to be wearing a vest."

"Hmm. I guess he didn't expect to face an armed opponent."

"That's my take. He'd have killed Dad, but when he failed with the first flurry of shots, he wasn't confident enough to continue the attack."

"Hard to explain a GSW to his distinguished guests tonight," Hammond said drily.

Seth felt a smile tug at his lips. "Yeah, a gunshot wound might be socially awkward."

Hammond sighed. "So what's the plan?"

"I haven't had a chance to plan," he admitted. "For tonight, we'll go back to Dad's house. If this was Winstead versus hired muscle, we should be safe tonight."

"What's your gut feeling?"

"He only said a word or two, but Robin seems sure that this time it was him. Hiring someone to grab the boy is one thing. You could claim the mother has gone on the run with him, and you're concerned for your son's safety. Hiring a killer is another story. From what she's said, Richard Winstead has a major ego problem. He'll need to kill her himself, not have it done secondhand."

"Can't argue," Hammond said, sounding weary.

After promising to keep each other updated, they left it at that. Seth returned to the waiting room, pausing in the doorway before Robin saw him. She looked exhausted, drained, although he knew the minute she saw him she'd go back to pretending she was fine.

His heart muscle cramped. She was beautiful to him even now, without makeup, with her hair unbrushed, without the spirit that had sparked his interest at that first meeting. He ached to see her truly relaxed and happy, teasing…or flushed and dazed with passion. The punch in his belly reminded him of how very vulnerable she was right now. He couldn't push.

He walked over to her, irritated when she straightened in the chair despite the sleeping weight of the boy and smoothed out the lines on her face.

"Sergeant Hammond hasn't found Winstead," Seth reported, lowering himself into a chair beside her. "Seems as if he's getting the runaround from staff and the senior partner in the law firm. He's determined that the small plane Winstead owns is not in the hangar, though. If he rented a car when he got down here, he did it under another name."

"That's sort of ironic," she said.

He smiled crookedly. "Yeah, it is. He could have asked for advice from you on how best to do it."

"Except I didn't do it well enough."

Seth let that go. Would he ever have met her if her latest identity had stood up to scrutiny? "According to the housekeeper, your ex is entertaining tonight at home," he said. "If that's true, he can't linger here in Oregon."

"Will we know?"

"Hammond is going to call the house, insist on speaking to him."

"Oh." Some of her tension slid away. "Then…then we don't have to worry tonight."

He laid a hand briefly over hers, balled on the arm of the chair. "I can't forget that he *wasn't* the one who tried to abduct Jacob. If you're sure?"

"Positive."

"Okay. That means we can't totally relax. Once I see Dad, though, we'll go back to the house. With some precautions, we should be fine."

What he'd really like was some backup, Seth thought. He wondered how soon he could get a security system installed, and whether he had to ask his father's permission first. *Probably*, he decided reluctantly.

"Tomorrow is Saturday. I can take the weekend off and then work from the house for a few days," he told Robin. "I'll make sure we have regular patrol drive-bys, too. I wish I knew how he got away so fast. The neighbor who heard the shots and called 9-1-1 didn't see or hear a vehicle. Unfortunately, nobody was at home in the house to the north of Dad's. Best guess, Winstead parked there."

"I know I'd have heard a car arriving. I was in the kitchen putting together some lunch. Except when I was out in back, I've always heard yours when you come home."

He captured her hand again. "Bet you never got that lunch, did you?"

Robin wrinkled her nose. "I've been feeling so sick about what happened, I'm just as glad I didn't eat. But when Jacob wakes up, he's going to be miserable."

"Just as well Dad hadn't eaten," Seth commented, "considering he had to be put under."

Worry darkened her eyes. "I didn't tell you he was having an attack of heartburn. I wanted to have him checked out at the ER, but he insists he's seen the doctor about it and is on medication. Did you know about it?"

"Hell, no!" Seth said, exasperated. "That's Dad for you. He doesn't want to admit any weakness. You must have caught him at a really bad moment, or he wouldn't have told you."

A tiny smile lit her face. "It could be a father-son thing, you know. Here you are, the young bull in the herd…"

He growled his opinion of that, although he suspected she saw his amusement. Yeah, she could be right. That sounded like Dad, too.

He heard his name just then, and insisted Robin bring Jacob through the swinging doors so that they weren't left exposed in the waiting room. The nurse found a chair for Robin, who told him to take his time.

He didn't need long, though. His father was surly about having to stay the night when he'd be perfectly fine at home. "What are you hanging around for?" he grumbled. "Where are Robin and Jacob?"

"Out in the hall."

"For God's sake, take them home!." He glared at Seth. "I don't need you hovering over me like a damn vulture."

Seth laughed. "I love you, too, Dad." He sobered. "Thank you for what you did today. For protecting those two when I couldn't."

"You know me better than that."

"I do." Seth gripped his father's hand. "I wanted to say it, anyway. If Robin had been killed, Jacob snatched—" Throat clogged, he couldn't finish, wasn't ready to say, *I'd have never gotten over it*. Ridiculous consid-

ering what a short time he'd known them…
but still true.

Never comfortable with talking about emotions, Dad snorted and said, "Get out of here."

Seth was reassured enough to do just that.

Chapter Twelve

A stop at a Dairy Queen after leaving the hospital improved Jacob's mood, and even Seth's, Robin thought. Maybe hers, too. French fries and ice cream fixed everything.

It was astonishing how quickly Michael's house had started to feel like home. Robin sighed with relief walking in—until she saw the torn wall in the hall just beyond the kitchen. These weren't just bullet holes, Seth explained, because a crime scene investigator had dug the bullets out of the wall. More blasé about it than she could be, he experimentally poked his fingers in one hole. His father had fired fewer shots, and had been more accurate, so presumably a couple were embedded in the intruder's Kevlar vest, while only one shot had nicked a corner of the kitchen island.

She stood looking around. "A shoot-out *here*." If she hadn't lived through it, she'd have thought it inconceivable—but then, she'd never expected to find a dead body in any place she lived, either.

Seth glanced at her. "It can happen any-where."

"Apparently. When I moved here, Lookout seemed so peaceful."

"Relatively speaking, it is. That's why the department needs only one detective. But we have burglaries, domestic abuse, assaults, drunkenness and ugly traffic accidents just like anyplace else."

And the occasional murder.

Seth had mentioned buying some Play-Doh, and now he said, "I need to cover that broken glass. Once I've done that, let's be artists."

Jacob liked watching Seth tack a piece of plywood he'd found in the barn over the upper half of the door. Robin tried to let Seth off the hook on the artist part—him buying the stuff in the first place was contribution enough—but he shook his head. "I need an excuse to play."

Lacking any artistic ability, Robin was intrigued to see how deftly he created a variety of animals before squishing them out of existence to form the next. Jacob concentrated hard and made a creature he called a "doggie" that was semirecognizable and not a whole lot cruder than her own efforts, which Seth eyed with amusement.

Jacob settled down then with his Tobbles, a toy that he seemed to find endlessly fascinating. He could make towers, nest the individual pieces, spin them and laugh uproariously when he knocked the whole thing down.

Seth made coffee for himself and Robin, calling to check on his father while it brewed.

"Asleep," he reported.

"During his whole career, he was never shot?" she asked, her guilt stirred again.

Seth shook his head, smiling. "Most cops aren't. A lot never fire their own gun, either. Some of it has to do with where you work, some with how good you are at de-escalating tense situations, but luck plays a big part, too."

"You wear one of those vests."

"I do, in part because I have been shot. Didn't feel good," he added.

Robin hated the image of a bullet penetrating his flesh, him falling back, bloody and stunned like his father had been. Still, she was curious. "Were you, I don't know, more nervous about doing your job afterward?"

He hesitated. "Nervous? No. More cautious? Yeah. It was a burglary in progress, and I'd left myself more exposed than I should have." He shrugged. "Live and learn."

Here she'd spent years with fear an ever-present companion, and Seth, who did a dangerous job, seemed blithe about the risks. Go figure.

He asked about her childhood, and she found herself sharing good times and bad. He opened up a little about losing his mother, probably because she'd just talked about her father's death and how hard it had been to accept.

"When she was first diagnosed, I was still at an age to have some swagger," Seth admitted. "On the job, I thought I could change the world. And why not? I'd never had big worries at home. Mom and Dad had a solid marriage, there were never any serious financial problems. I won't say Grace and I were spoiled, but maybe close. As a kid, I thought my dad was a real hero, invincible."

And he was, until *she* had come along, Robin couldn't help thinking.

She said quietly, "Today he really was a hero. I'll always see him that way."

"Yeah." Seth cleared his throat. "Yeah." After a minute, he said, "Seeing him break down after Mom's diagnosis, that really shook me. Of course she'd get better! My family was golden, right? Why wouldn't he have faith?"

"He knew more than you did."

His rueful gaze met hers. "Probably. To Grace and me, my parents tried to sound upbeat. Mom's chemotherapy was going great. Sure, she lost her hair, but that summer was hot, and she bragged about how cool it was. Not having to wash, dry, style hair was a bonus. Maybe she'd stick to wigs and not bother growing her hair out again. She admitted to occasional nausea, but nowhere near as bad as she'd expected." Seth gazed at the front window, seeing the past instead of the present, Robin guessed. "I was still living in Portland," he continued. "Never occurred to me to wonder if I was getting the whole story. Until *wham*. Dad told me he was taking retirement. Mom had decided to refuse any more treatments. They weren't working, and all they did was make her miserable."

Robin reached across the sofa cushion separating them and took his hand. He grabbed on hard, sinews standing out on his forearm.

"I hadn't been home in weeks." His mouth twisted. "Too busy, you know."

"Because your parents didn't *want* you to feel that they needed you," she pointed out.

"God forbid they be a burden on me."

"Seth." She waited until he was looking at her. "It's also possible they needed that time with just the two of them. If you'd insisted on coming home to help sooner, you might have robbed them of a chance to appreciate each other and...say goodbye."

He stared at her, unblinking. Finally, his shoulders loosened and he let out a heavy sigh. "Maybe."

"And you came when they did need you," she said gently.

"Yeah." One corner of his mouth curled. "Thank you." And he lifted her hand to his mouth.

The lingering kiss on her knuckles sent tingles up her arm. She hadn't known how sensitive the skin there was.

Or maybe Seth made her whole body sensitive.

Jacob came over for a cuddle and wanted a snack. Robin peeled and cut up carrots and celery, setting out peanut butter and cream cheese for dips. She discovered that Seth liked peanut butter as much as her two-year-old did, but at least *he* didn't smear it all over his face.

He had to take several phone calls that she gathered had to do with other investigations. Robin decided the late-afternoon DQ meal wouldn't hold them until bedtime, and put potatoes and eggs on to boil for a potato salad.

Jacob was getting whiny and tired by the time the salad was ready to eat. She plopped him into the high chair with a toddler-size serving while she also made a fruit salad.

Seth had gone outside to talk, and she heard his phone ring one more time before he came in.

"That was Hammond. Your ex is definitely home. He claims to have flown to Spokane today. Of course he refused to name the client he supposedly met with. Attorney-client privilege." He shook his head. "I'll bet he has some whopping bruises on his chest."

She stopped halfway between the refrigerator and the table. "Really?"

"Oh, yeah. Bullets don't penetrate the vest, but that doesn't mean the impact isn't tremendous. You can end up with broken ribs or collarbone, too."

"I can only hope," Robin said acidly.

He smiled faintly. "I was thinking the same thing."

After cleaning up Jacob's face, she gave him a piece of cantaloupe to gnaw on and squish. She and Seth sat down to eat. Jacob started squirming long before Robin finished her meal, so she washed his hands and face again and set him down. Seth put on a video of cartoons for him and came back to the table.

"He's winding down."

"Yes. I'm glad he didn't see more today, and didn't understand what was happening."

"Me, too. How are *you* holding up?"

OF COURSE SHE was fine.

Seth snorted. "I don't buy that. *I'm* not fine. I came home to find my father bleeding on the floor. I saw that bullet hole above the stairs. How close did that come to you?"

She swallowed. "Too close. If not for your father—" The knuckles of her hand holding the fork gleamed white.

"Then quit pretending with me, okay?" He shouldn't snap at her, but he'd been all over the emotional map today. The least she could give him was honesty.

Her temper sparked. "That's not really fair. I'm a single mother. For Jacob, I can't let myself surrender to emotion or the flu or anything else. I'm not in the habit of whining, anyway."

Had she stayed with a vicious man longer than she had to because she couldn't bring herself to ask for help? Seth was smart enough not to say that out loud. She was right, anyway; he wasn't being fair. He thought his problem was that he wanted to know she trusted him. Did he want her to throw herself in his arms so he could feel manly?

Probably, although he might not respect her as much if she weren't a woman who pulled herself up after every near-disaster and did what she had to do. Even if that was, occasionally, trying to take off in the middle of the night to go it alone.

"You're right," he said gruffly. "I'm sorry."

"Why do you suppose Richard called me?" she asked abruptly. "He couldn't have really believed I'd just hand over Jacob."

Seth forced himself to shift gears, to consider her question logically. "You so sure about that? He may be incapable of understanding maternal love. Or any love, for that matter."

"I suppose that's true." She pushed back from the table. "I need to put Jacob to bed. If you're not done eating—"

"I'll put the leftovers away." Would she come back down, or go to bed herself, however ridiculously early the hour? He didn't ask. It might be best if he didn't see her again this evening. His control felt shaky.

She nodded and left the kitchen. He heard her soft voice and then footsteps on the stairs.

Seth had another helping of potato salad, called to check on his father again and started clearing the table. The whole time, he pictured Robin upstairs. Kissing her son good-night.

Brushing her teeth, washing her face...getting ready to take a shower?

He listened, but didn't hear water running. Changing into pajamas, then.

He closed the dishwasher door and stiffened at the sound of footsteps on the stairs again. She appeared in the doorway.

"I don't know if I can actually sleep yet. I keep thinking...you know."

Seth knew.

"I thought I might watch TV or find a book."

"You don't have to ask permission." He dried his hands. "Why don't you pick out a download of a show if you see anything that appeals to you? I wouldn't mind watching a movie."

"Okay." She vanished into the living room.

Seth squeezed the tight muscles in his neck. A quiet evening with only the two of them could tempt him into doing something he shouldn't. After the brutality of her marriage, Robin might not be ready for a physical relationship with a man. Disturbed by the reminder, he turned off the overhead light in the kitchen and followed her.

She sat cross-legged on the floor in front of the television with the remote, flipping through the options. Hearing him, she looked over her shoulder. "It's been years since I've watched many movies. Richard—" She shook off that memory. "Since then I haven't had the energy."

"I can see why, with your living 6:30 a.m. alarm."

She smiled. "Is there something you want to watch?"

You.

"Maybe something on TV if you'd rather." He hesitated. "Or we can talk, or sit here in dead silence. Whatever you'd prefer."

After a minute she nodded, rose gracefully to her feet and approached the couch as warily as an antelope nearing a watering hole shared with a pride of lions.

He made a move to stand. "Would you rather be alone?"

"No. I mean, if there's something else you'd rather be doing…"

Seth smiled gently. "There's nothing." He relaxed at one end of the couch and lifted his arm. "Come here."

She came, melting into him as naturally as if they spent every evening like this—which he'd like to do. Seth cuddled her close and bent to rub his cheek against her hair. With his jaw bristly, strands of her hair clung to his face.

"Hey," he said, lifting his head. "Your hair is growing out."

"Out?" Robin sat up, clapping a hand to the top of her head. "You mean the color?"

"Yep. Let me see." He waited until she dropped her hand and scrutinized the quarter of an inch—if that—of auburn roots. "You'll let it grow out, won't you?"

"No!" She twisted toward him in alarm, before blinking. "Well… I guess I can. You know, I was planning to go with light brown next."

He tapped a forefinger on the freckles scattered over the bridge of her nose. "You're a redhead, whether you like it or not." Damn, the huskiness in his voice would tell her what he was thinking.

If she couldn't already.

"Seth?" she whispered.

He cupped her jaw and cheek both, tracing her lips with his thumb. "Yeah?"

"Would you kiss me?"

He made a hoarse sound and obliged. The instant she parted her lips, his tongue drove inside. If hers hadn't stroked his, twined around it, he might have retreated. As it was, the kiss quickly became deep and passionate. He kneaded the back of her neck, slid his other hand up her rib cage until it rested just beneath her breast.

When he lifted his mouth from hers for a quick breath, she scrambled onto his lap. Seth caught one glimpse of her face, cheeks flushed, eyes dreamy. Body surging, he repositioned her so that she straddled him. The tight clasp of her thighs drove him wild.

As the kiss became hungrier, he heard a low moan that had to have come from her throat. The sound ratcheted up his arousal. His evening beard must be scratching her skin, but if so she couldn't mind too much.

She squirmed on him and his hips rocked involuntarily. He slid a hand beneath the hem of her shirt and stroked her back, finding the sharp edges of her shoulder blades, the delicate string of vertebrae. He squeezed her waist, wanting to get his hand between them but unwilling to give up the pleasure of feeling the soft pressure of her breasts against his chest.

Damn, he wished she wasn't wearing pants. He kneaded her butt, nipped her lower lip. Desperation drove him to tear his mouth from hers.

"Robin, let me—"

Her stare held no comprehension.

"I want you."

"Yes," she whispered, and rocked forward and back until he was in acute pain.

A harsh groan escaped him. "No, we need to—"

What? Have sex right here on the sofa? With him distracted, they'd be vulnerable if someone shattered glass again and entered the house fast. He realized he'd quit paying attention to sounds from outside.

At least upstairs he'd have a warning.

"My bedroom," he said.

Her lashes fluttered. Was that uncertainty he saw on her face? Having to ask that question forced him to recall his own reservations. He made himself lift her off his thighs and set her beside him on the couch.

"Robin," he said again, gruffly. "I told myself I wouldn't put you in this position."

"This...*position*?"

Seth swore and lifted a shaky hand to scrub over his face. "You're depending on me to keep you safe. If you have any mixed feelings..."

Her spine stiffened and her chin jutted. "You think I'd go to bed with you if I really had reservations?"

Her tone told him he'd insulted her without intending to.

"That's not—"

"It is." Anger and hurt blazed in her eyes. "*I* asked you to kiss me."

He glared at her.

Robin jumped up.

Seth stood, too, and reached for one of her hands. "I just didn't want you to feel compromised."

There was surprise on her face, but hurt was still there, too.

"What I said is about me. Cops have to be extra careful. I thought you were under enough pressure. That...what I feel for you could wait." He grimaced. "Except, once I kiss you, I forget about doing the right thing."

Shoulders still stiff, she said, "I'm an adult, Seth. I don't know what will happen with Richard. Tonight feels like we're in the eye of the hurricane. Everything is still swirling around, but here, now, we're safe. I'm attracted to you. This...feels new to me. I was afraid I'd lose my chance if I let the moment pass by."

"I'm sorry." He leaned forward to rest his forehead on hers.

"Let's not look for excuses," she said softly, nuzzling him. "Maybe this isn't the right time."

He jerked his head up. "Don't say that. I

was trying to be...scrupulous. But the truth is I've been aching for you, Robin."

She took long enough to search his face that he was afraid she would back off. A nerve jerked in his cheek. Yeah, he wanted her desperately, but he didn't know why he felt so much was riding on her decision now. There'd be a later.

But a tight, uncomfortable knot in his chest made him remember what happened to his father today. Half an inch to the right, and the shot that grazed Dad's head would have killed him. The bullet hole above the staircase told him how easily Robin might have been wounded if not killed, too. He could have lost either or both today.

I was afraid I'd lose my chance if I let the moment pass by.

She was right. Tomorrow, anything could happen. He needed tonight.

THERE REALLY WASN'T any decision at all. Robin understood why Seth had worried that she might feel pressured. It was right for a man with his sense of integrity. She'd gotten mad, but really he'd been trying to protect her. Again.

She stepped forward, smile tremulous. "Good."

His arms came around her hard. She held on tightly, too.

"Will you go up to my bedroom?" he asked, voice rough. "Let me do a last check down here."

"Okay." She let go, feeling his equal reluctance as he released her. "Hurry."

Robin dashed upstairs, pausing only to release the spring-loaded gate at the top and reattach it when she was on the other side. Along with corralling Jacob, it would slow down an intruder.

She rushed to the bathroom to brush her teeth before tiptoeing into her bedroom to check on Jacob. Sometimes he curled into a tight ball to sleep; other times, like now, he sprawled in a careless way that made it easy to picture the future when her little boy would be taller than her, with a deep voice and whiskers.

She cocked her head. Had she heard a bell tinkling? That was strange. Robin tugged Jacob's covers higher and then stepped out of the bedroom to find Seth coming down the hall toward her, his eyes locked in on hers.

Her mouth dried. Just like that, she was a woman, not a mother. His purposeful stride was pure male, predatory in a good way.

He glanced past her into the guest room. "Asleep?" he murmured.

She nodded. "I heard something."

He nudged her a few steps down the hall and into his bedroom, dominated by a king-size bed. "I tied bells to doorknobs downstairs and to both child gates."

"You set up the one at the bottom, too?"

"I did." His voice was as intense as his eyes. "I want you to feel safe."

"To be able to think about nothing but you."

"Yes."

"I can do that," she whispered, and he kissed her, possessive, greedy...and tender.

Chapter Thirteen

Seth steered her to his bed, where he turned on a lamp. Robin was briefly jarred from the mood when he reached behind his back and produced a handgun that he set on the bedside stand.

Then, instead of kissing her, he began slowly undressing her. After pulling her shirt off over her head, he unhooked her bra. Robin wriggled her shoulders so the straps slid off and the bra dropped to her feet. He stopped for a long moment, his eyes heated as he looked. Matching desire lit coals low in her belly.

She wanted to see him, too. He stood still while she unbuttoned his shirt, but took over to shrug out of it and toss it away. He was beautiful with those wide shoulders and powerful chest, defined muscles that tightened and jerked when she splayed her hands on him and explored. Finding the circle of puckered skin on his side below his ribs, she paused for a brief moment of combined fear and thankfulness that he'd survived. He lasted a whole minute or two, then said, "I want you naked."

They stripped in record time, her able to kick off her slip-ons, Seth having to kneel to untie his boots. She heard a thud when one hit a wall. While he was unbuttoning his trousers, Robin pulled back the covers and crawled onto the bed.

In seconds, he was with her, over her. Kissing her with such tenderness, her bones seemed to dissolve. At last he kissed his way down her throat, rubbed a scratchy cheek on her chest and then reared up to take her nipple into his mouth. She cried out, whimpering when she felt the rhythmic pull all the way to her toes. She kneaded what she could reach of his back. Weight on his elbow, he switched to the other breast.

By the time he returned to her mouth, Robin was desperate. Her fingers dug into those strong muscles as she tried to pull him closer. She wanted him inside her with unfamiliar urgency, but if anything he slowed down, stroking her body and finding every sensitive spot, until finally his fingers slid between her legs.

Her back spasmed into an arch as she felt herself tightening, tightening. "Please," she heard herself say. "Now."

He was there, pressing against her, when suddenly he lurched away.

She heard a ripping sound and within seconds, he was back, seating himself deep with a long thrust. And then he did it again, and again, and her body instinctively matched his pace.

This felt glorious, and yet she was frantic, too. She didn't have to chase an orgasm; it slammed into her. Even as she spasmed, he made a guttural sound and went rigid.

When he sagged down on her, he rolled, taking her with him. Robin ended up with her head on his shoulder, where she could both feel and hear his racing heartbeat. She laid her hand right atop his heart, where it seemed to belong.

And then a chill trickled through her bloodstream. She'd been afraid he wouldn't trust her if she told him all her secrets, but her silence suddenly felt wrong.

She had to tell him everything…but not now. It wouldn't be so terrible if she waited, would it?

He planned to work from home for a few

days, so she could talk to him in the morning. Give herself the rest of the night. Soak up all the memories she could, in case his reaction to her confessions was what she expected. Of course he wouldn't be able to ignore the things she'd done...and not done.

But he was hers for tonight.

HOLDING ROBIN CLOSE, stunned, Seth knew he should say something but had no idea what. The thoughts he was having were wildly premature.

"That was amazing," he said after a moment.

Robin murmured something indecipherable.

Apparently she hadn't taken offense, because they made love twice more during the night, and, having awakened to the gray light of dawn, Seth had just cupped his hands around her breasts when a perplexed "Mommy?" came from the hall.

"Damn," he muttered.

Robin shot up, disheveled and disoriented, clutching the covers. "What? Where—Jacob?"

"Bright-eyed and bushy-tailed."

"Jacob?" Robin breathed. "Seth, I don't suppose you can reach any of my clothes."

"Uh..." Seth leaned over the edge of the bed

and was able to snag her panties and jeans. And, stretching, his shirt.

"I'm in here," she called.

"Mommy?" Jacob appeared, wafting the smell of urine. "The bed is wet."

"I can handle this," Seth suggested. Beneath the covers, he yanked on his knit boxers, then swung his feet to the floor and stood. "How about I start you a bath while Mommy gets dressed?"

"Yeah!" Jacob snagged his hand.

Seth grinned over his shoulder at Robin, who still looked discombobulated.

An hour later, the sense of happiness and optimism he'd started the day with had waned. He'd known that sleeping with Robin would change their relationship. How could it not? What he hadn't expected was her to shut him out.

Her smiles were polite and didn't reach her eyes. She jumped up and left the table when Jacob finished eating. Seth was left to finish alone. When he wandered after them to the living room, she concentrated her attention on Jacob. Tiny worry lines scored her forehead. She kept her distance, pretending not to notice when he held out a hand to her.

She did focus on him after he called the hospital. "Will they let your dad come home today?"

"He needs to wait to see the doctor around eleven. He says the nurse thinks he'll be released."

"Oh. Oh, that's good."

Jacob tugged at her shirt. "Mommy, look!"

She admired the tower he'd built and clapped when he toppled it.

Feeling invisible, Seth went back to the kitchen and poured another cup of coffee.

What was going on? He'd swear the night had been as good for her as it was for him, so why would she regret anything about it?

Brooding wouldn't help, so Seth opened his laptop and went online to check his email. He scanned the list. Nothing new from Hammond. Had the sergeant been able to leave an officer watching Winstead's house? Likely not, given the usual budgetary restraints.

His phone rang, a county deputy letting him know that two houses on the outskirts of town had been broken into during the night and the usual electronics, wallets and jewelry taken.

"Fits the profile," the frustrated deputy reported. "One couple was out of town. It was a neighbor who saw the back door open and called. The other family slept through the intrusion."

Frowning, Seth tipped his chair back on two legs. "They've been careful so far *not* to enter homes when people are there."

"Method of entry was the same."

Mostly flimsy back-door locks had been jimmied. Why did people bother with dead bolts on the front if they were going to make it so easy to break into their houses through other doors or windows? Seth particularly disliked exterior doors that had glass panes. Witness yesterday's break-in here. He had so far been unable to persuade his father to replace the damn door, although he'd already made up his mind to do it without asking permission.

"You going to try for fingerprints?" he asked now.

"Captain says yes. He's ticked."

"I am, too. Haven't heard yet, but I'll let you know if anyplace in town got hit last night."

As he set down the phone, he saw Robin hesitating just inside the kitchen. Jacob was settled in watching a movie.

"Are you busy?" she asked.

"No." He nodded at the chair across the table. "Coffee?"

"I think I'll pour myself some water."

She did so and sat down. He could only

call her expression bleak. "There are…things I haven't told you."

No kidding. He raised his eyebrows while keeping his mouth shut.

Her gaze slid away. "I should have told you before we…" She stole a look at his face.

"I'm listening."

She shifted in place, moistened her lips and blurted, "I killed a man."

The front legs of his chair crashed back to the floor. *"What?"*

"I think I killed him," Robin said more softly.

"You think."

"I didn't hang around to be sure, okay?"

Seth stared at her. "Start at the beginning."

Hot spots of color on her cheeks and tightly clasped hands betrayed how artificial her calm was. "It was after the divorce. When I saw the chance to sneak out of Richard's house, there wasn't time to go back for anything. I didn't care about clothes or… But I kept some things that were important to me in a box on the shelf in the closet."

He didn't like where this was going.

"I read online that Richard would be away for a few days, on some kind of conference in San Francisco. I chose a day the housekeeper would be off. I'd have been out of luck if he'd changed the gate code and lock, but he hadn't, so I let myself in. The house was completely silent." Her throat worked. "I hurried upstairs and felt so lucky to find the box where I'd left it. I grabbed it, but when I turned around, *he* was there."

"The bodyguard," Seth guessed. Dread filled his stomach.

"Yes. I'm sorry, I do know his name. It's— it was—Brad McCormick. He gave me this nasty smile and said, 'The boss knew what he was talking about. Here you are, right on time.' And then he grabbed me and started dragging me toward the door." Her voice wobbled.

"Robin."

Naked anguish in her eyes, she said, "Let me finish."

He managed a nod.

"I dropped the box on the bed. I was fixated on not letting anything get broken, which sounds stupid, but—" She hunched her shoulders. "I fought. He…seemed to enjoy it. I thought he might rape me."

He wasn't sure he was capable of speech.

"I managed to scramble away enough to get my hands on the lamp. The base was wrought iron and stained glass, and it was really heavy. I hit him in the head and he just…fell over. I picked up my box because if I didn't anyone would know I'd been there, and I left. Waiting for the bus, I was shaking and my teeth were chattering and I knew I should call 9-1-1 in case he *wasn't* dead, but how could I? So I didn't do anything, which is one more thing to feel guilty about."

"He assaulted you." He didn't recognize his own voice.

"But I was trespassing. With the divorce final, I didn't have any right to be there."

Seth shook his head. "You should have been able to pack the things that were important to you when you told your husband that the marriage was over."

She let out a shuddery breath that might have been a sob. "I did have a social worker call and ask him for the small things that were important to me. She offered to meet him. He laughed and hung up on her."

"So you tried doing it the civilized way." Was he making excuses for her? Seth discovered he didn't care.

Robin squeezed her hands together so hard it had to be painful. "I watched the newspaper. I kept expecting to get arrested. But the police never came, and I never saw anything about the death in the paper or online."

"I can't believe Winstead wouldn't have

accused you if he found his employee dead in the master bedroom." He hesitated. "Were there surveillance cameras?"

Shock slowly altered her face. "I...don't know."

"You might have only knocked him out, you know."

"I hoped, but I hit him hard. There was a lot of blood." She closed her eyes. "I've been so afraid ever since then that I'd be arrested and convicted and *he'd* get Jacob."

Unable to sit still any longer, Seth shoved his chair back. "I swear that won't happen." His commitment to the letter of the law had just been supplanted by something more important.

"How can you promise that?"

"Unless he has time-and date-stamped footage showing you entering the house, how can he prove you were there? That you hit this Brad McCormick over the head? There could have been burglars in the house. He could have been in his boss's bedroom because he was in league with them, only there was a falling out." Seth stalked toward the patio door.

She protested, "But my fingerprints would be on the lamp!"

He swung around. "Sure they were. You

shared that bedroom for two years. The surprise would be if your prints *weren't* on the thing."

"The housekeeper…"

"Dusting doesn't remove fingerprints."

Robin's headshake looked dazed. "If I hadn't already known I was pregnant, I would have gone to the police. I hope you believe that."

He went to her and crouched beside her. "You have to know I do," he said roughly.

Her eyes shimmered. "There's something else you need to know." She became fascinated with the the tabletop.

Seth stood, looking down at her. In this light, he could see the auburn roots of her hair better. It made her look vulnerable, as if she'd quit protecting herself from him.

"Will you sit down?" she asked timidly.

Was she *afraid* of his reaction? Hating to think that, he confined himself to a nod. He walked to the doorway first to reassure himself that Jacob was okay. The boy seemed engrossed by the Disney movie.

Then he forced himself to sit across the table from Robin again. Her face was as colorless as he'd ever seen it. Against that backdrop, her eyes were dark and bruised.

"I've mentioned my sister."

He braced himself.

"A FEW YEARS AGO, Allie—short for Allison—was diagnosed with a kidney disease called glomerulonephritis. Doctors don't know what caused it. A lot of the common triggers don't apply to her. It turned out she had only one kidney." Keeping her gaze deliberately unfocused so she didn't have to see Seth's reaction, Robin kept to a near-monotone. "She had to move home. At first she kept working, but she couldn't when she started dialysis. I was still married when her doctor started talking about a transplant. I got tested and was a match."

Of course, Seth had seen her torso and knew she had no scar from surgery.

"When Richard found out I'd been tested, he flipped out. His wife wasn't giving away a body part. He seemed repulsed by the idea that I'd be left with a scar." She took a deep breath. "I had already made up my mind to leave him, and Allie wasn't desperate."

"But by the time you were free, you knew you were pregnant."

"Yes." When the pregnancy test came up positive, she felt so conflicted that it was like the shocking aftermath of a car accident. She had to be sure she could love this baby, Richard's child. Feeling in her heart that she could came as a huge relief. Guilt was in the mix, because Allie was counting on her, ebullient with hope, and now Robin wouldn't be accepted as a kidney donor for nearly a year.

She went on, "Her kidney has continued to fail. They've searched for another donor, but have not found anyone." She made herself meet Seth's eyes. "I could have done it, but I was afraid to go back to Seattle. Afraid Richard would find out. My mother wouldn't be able to stand up to him to keep Jacob safe." She made herself look at him, see a hard gaze out of eyes gone a turbulent blue. Focusing on her hands, she finished in a voice barely above a whisper. "I'm the only person who can save her, and I won't. Allie must hate me. It's…one reason I don't call home more often."

There. Now he knew, and would despise her.

Only… Seth had circled the table and picked her up as effortlessly as if she were a child. He sat down, Robin on his lap, cradled within the solid strength of his arms. She buried her face against his chest so he couldn't see it.

"I do not believe your sister hates you."

He sounded so gentle, Robin felt a tremble deep inside, as if a fault line was shifting.

"We know that Richard has hunted long and hard for you. He has to have spent a fortune paying investigators. Do you think for a *minute* that he wouldn't be watching your mother and sister? That if she were to go in for surgery, he wouldn't know?"

No. She didn't think that. He wasn't just abusive. It had become increasingly obvious that beneath the surface he was an obsessive, crazy man.

"Would Allie be happy to have a new kidney if you died giving it to her?"

"But I wouldn't necessarily—"

"If Winstead had a shot at you, I think you would," he said. "Is your sister still eligible for a kidney?"

Robin bobbed her head.

"Then there's time for you to give her one. I'd rather bring that creep down first, but if this drags on, we'll go to Seattle and I'll make damn sure nothing goes wrong, for you, your sister or Jacob. Do you hear me?"

It took her a minute to regain enough composure to raise her head. He meant it, every word.

That movement inside, the fault line, cracked wide open. Robin had always known she *could* love him. She just hadn't imagined it could happen from one second to the next and be so painful. Remembering what he'd said about his younger self, she thought, *He still has that swagger.* She believed he'd try to keep his promise, but how would she live with herself if he died?

HE'D LIKE TO THINK he had gotten good at reading what Robin was thinking, but there'd been the one moment, an expression Seth didn't understand. Hope, disbelief, fear. Taken together, what did it mean?

He shook the worry off and concentrated on his search, eliminating the Brad or Bradley McCormicks not the right age, who'd never lived in the Seattle area, who didn't meet the description Robin gave him. Why didn't anyone of that name appear on the list of Winstead's former and current employees that Hammond had forwarded to Seth?

An alternative name caught his eye: Braedon McCormick. Seth tugged at the string. This McCormick had been in the army, deployed twice to Iraq, then went to work as a deputy in Lewis County south of Seattle. Didn't last long there, although Seth couldn't determine whether he'd been fired or quit. Following his brief stint in law enforcement, he became an investigator with a somewhat sketchy-seeming PI firm. His name popped up a couple more times…and that was it. Seth tried every option he could think of, concluding at last that only two likely reasons for the disappearance existed. Number one, Braedon had moved out of state; it could be tedious trying to pull up a driver's license or PI license application in another state. Number two, he was dead, albeit with no fanfare. No investigation into his death, no obituary, no funeral.

Seth listened to the clatter from the kitchen where Robin was putting together lunch. Dad would be showing up any minute; one of his buddies from his cop days was giving him a ride home.

Seth stretched as he debated calling Hammond to talk about this McCormick guy. There was a lot he didn't want to say, but a Seattle PD officer might be able to find something Seth couldn't.

While he was still waffling, his phone rang. Hammond.

"Renner here," he answered.

"Thought I'd let you know Winstead is staying put for the moment," the sergeant said. "Real conspicuously. Went out for a fancy breakfast this morning with a female tech executive, then stopped by city hall where he somehow corralled a journalist to give a statement about a proposed referendum. Last report, he went to Palisade for a waterfront lunch with one of the mayor's assistants."

"Pricey?"

"Very," Hammond said drily. "Gotta wonder what his plans are for dinner."

"Listen, Ms. Hollis remembers a man who worked for Richard who isn't on your list. Last name McCormick. He went by Brad, but I think his legal first name is Braedon." He shared what he'd learned about the man.

"He might technically still have been working for the PI outfit," Hammond said. "Does Ms. Hollis think he could have been the one who grabbed her kid?"

No, she thinks the guy is dead wasn't something Seth was prepared to share.

"That's a possibility. He was a sometime-driver for Winstead, but she thought he was more of a bodyguard." He hesitated. "During the months while she was trying to find an opportunity to leave the bastard, this McCormick was always there, watching her."

"All right," Hammond said readily. "I'll start digging."

Question was: Would he unearth a body?

Chapter Fourteen

Robin shut the bathroom door in Michael's face, wishing it had more than one of those useless little push-button locks that could be opened with a bobby pin. *Jacob* could probably pop it.

Not that Michael would try. No, he'd just linger where he'd be sure to see her when she came out.

That seemed to be the Renner men's plan: keep an eye on her at all times. Since Jacob also tended to trail her, she was about ready to go seriously crazy.

She closed the toilet seat and sat down, digging her fingers into her hair and tugging. What would they do if she didn't come out?

Fiddle that stupid lock to open the door, that's what. In Michael's case, he'd act solicitous, be anxious to know why she felt compelled to hide. Seth would just give her a smoldering look that said he was as frustrated as she was. And yes, sexual frustration definitely contributed to her mood. There was no way that she and Seth could make love again in this house with his father home. And where would they go that they couldn't be followed? Outside, where anyone could walk right up to them? Head to his house, leaving Jacob vulnerable with only an injured man to guard him?

She and Seth hadn't talked about it. The closest they came was the first night after Michael was released from the hospital, when Seth walked her to her bedroom door and murmured, "Damn, I want to haul you off to my bed."

She'd squeezed her thighs together in a futile effort to stifle the powerful bolt of need.

Yesterday, during Jacob's naptime, Seth all but dragged her outside and around the corner of the house where he could kiss her until she was limp. Then he'd escorted her back to the deck where he gave her updates from his contact at Seattle PD.

He'd probably wanted to kiss her before giving her the bad news. Braedon McCormick had vanished within a time frame that fit with her having caved in his head.

"There's a lot that's hinky about it, though," Seth had added. "Why wouldn't Winstead have reported the death, if in fact he came home to find this guy dead? If your ex suspected you, he could have gotten you in trouble, which I'd expect him to enjoy. If he'd called 9-1-1 without mentioning you, SPD would have investigated the death under the assumption there'd been an intruder. I doubt they'd have considered him a suspect. Instead, it's looking as if he buried the body or dumped it in the Sound."

She didn't get it, either, although she repeatedly mulled over something else Seth had thrown out. What if she *hadn't* killed Brad McCormick? Furious because his trusted employee had screwed up, her ex-husband could have finished the job, but realized he'd likely left forensic evidence that would give him away.

She'd seen Richard's icy rage when an employee hadn't jumped high enough when he snapped his fingers. Yes, he was capable of murder in a temper as well as killing in cold blood—or, as the law put it, with malice aforethought. Say, an ex-wife who'd had no business leaving him.

With a sigh, she finally gave up and left her bathroom refuge to find Seth and Michael engaged in what appeared to be an intense conversation in the kitchen. Seth broke off midsentence, and both their heads turned the instant she appeared.

"You okay?" Seth asked.

"I'm fine." She'd chosen his least favorite words in the world.

His jaw muscles knotted.

She crossed her arms. "What were you two talking about?"

"Making plans," he said shortly.

"While I was safely out of earshot?"

His mouth tightened.

"You know the smartest thing would be for Jacob and I to go somewhere Richard couldn't find us. You could help me."

"Not an option," he said curtly.

"Why?"

"You need to be free to live when and where you choose. To use your real name." He glanced at his father then back to her. "To get medical care, visit your mother and sister."

She thought he was done. He wasn't.

"Get married."

Robin gaped at him. Was he implying…? Her heart felt as if it was playing hopscotch.

Had she imagined that slight nod?

After a moment, she said in a low voice, "I know you're right. But your dad was hurt because of us, and if it happened again, to either of you—" She couldn't finish, couldn't say, *If either of you died.* She couldn't forgive herself for that, either.

"Hey." Seth stepped forward and tipped her chin up. "Don't worry so much." He bent his head and kissed her lightly.

It was the first time he'd done anything like that in front of his father, who had been a silent spectator to the scene. Had Michael already figured out that something was going on between them? Or had Seth told him?

She backed away. "I'd better…um…" Spend some time with her son. That was it. She said so, and fled.

SETH COULDN'T HELP wondering why Winstead was so obviously keeping the world apprised of what he was doing and where he was doing it. He might as well be buying billboard space up and down I-5 between Seattle and Portland.

Now, if Robin was wrong in believing that the guy's ego would demand he kill her himself, his current public busyness made sense. With him so easy to track, he might think Robin and the police would relax. A hired gun could stroll right in and take care of her. With Winstead's alibi well-established, he could go straight to court demanding custody of his son.

As things stood, he'd get it, a truth that

burned like acid in Seth's gut. He had seriously considered suggesting a quick marriage to Robin so he'd have some legal claim on Jacob, but that wouldn't give him any certainty of winning a custody battle, even with Robin's medical records to show the judge. Didn't matter that Winstead had never met Jacob, when he had the argument that the child's mother had never given him the chance.

He heard the rumble of an engine before he saw a large panel truck coming up his father's driveway. Right on time. Seth went out to meet the lumberyard driver and help unload the door he had ordered. Installing it would give him something to do this afternoon.

Given the thump the door made when he leaned it against the clapboard wall, he wasn't surprised to let himself in to find Robin hovering.

"I'm replacing the door," he said.

A smile played at the corners of her mouth and lit eyes that had been shadowed too often since he'd met her. "I don't know if I want to stick around to hear the fireworks or not."

He turned on hearing the thunder of small, sock-clad feet. Jacob, coming to find out what was up. Seth squatted and the boy threw himself into his arms, allowing Seth to rise easily and swing him in the air. He chortled and held out his arms as if he was flying. He'd taken to galloping to find Seth half a dozen times a day so he could "fly."

Laughing with him, Seth felt a clutch beneath the breastbone. It was a credit to Robin that the boy had such an open, winning personality despite the ongoing fear she'd lived with. Seeing her in his freckled face didn't hurt, either. Seth wouldn't at all mind this kid calling him "Daddy."

Yeah, he was a goner, and twice over.

"Gotta do some work, buddy," he said, when he set Jacob down.

Robin took the boy's hand. "Do you need to go potty?"

"No!" Jacob insisted. "No, no, no, no!"

"Uh-oh." Seth grinned at her. "The terrible twos may be upon us. Ah…where's Dad?"

"While you were outside, he took a pain pill. He said he thought he'd lie down for a while."

Seth grunted. "Why does everybody say, 'I'm fine' when it's a lie?"

"Gee, I don't know. Maybe as an alternative to whining?"

Laughing, he caught her close for a kiss.

Robin laughed and blushed, too.

Seth was able to remove the old door without a lot of racket. He was tapping a shim in place while installing the new one when Dad stomped into the kitchen.

"Did you forget this is *my* house?" he demanded.

"Nope." Seth tested the swing of the door and decided he could go ahead and replace the molding and install the new dead bolt. "What? You wanted me to put in a new pane of glass as an invitation to break in?"

His father glowered. "I keep my weapon close."

Seth narrowed his eyes. "Sure, but normally in a gun safe. You need the house to be secure enough that you have time to dial the combination and get the damn gun out. And I've decided I'd had enough of this argument."

With a snort that sounded like a bull about to charge, his dad stalked out.

"He's mad at you," Robin said after a minute.

Seth smiled. "Not really. It's all bluster and fury."

"Butting heads is more like it."

ROBIN HEARD THE shower running in the master bedroom bath when she slipped out into the hall after tucking in Jacob. Michael must be getting ready for an early bedtime. He'd tried to hide how much he was hurting today, but she'd been able to tell. The physical therapist he'd seen yesterday wanted him doing a set of exercises twice a day. Robin tried to stay out of sight when he did them so he didn't feel as if he had to stifle all the pained sounds. She'd noticed Seth doing the same.

Tonight, when she started downstairs, Seth was waiting for her at the foot. His eyes never left her. He might as well have been touching her, given the way her body activated in response.

"Thought Jacob would never go to sleep," he mumbled, and kissed her.

That's all it took for Robin to forget about her son upstairs, never mind Seth's father. She flung her arms around Seth's neck and rose on tiptoe so he didn't have to bend over so far.

He solved that problem by lifting her until she could wrap her legs around his waist and ride his erection. Groaning, he carried her to the kitchen, where he lowered her to the granite top on the island. His hands were free to rove, and she could still clasp her ankles behind his back and rub against him.

Seth raised his head once and seemed to be listening before he dived back in with a kiss that was all raw need. Within seconds, Robin quit thinking. Here and now was good. Who needed to breathe?

She managed to squeeze a hand between them to unbutton his jeans and fumble for the zipper tab.

Seth wrenched his mouth away from hers and reached down to grab her hand. "Not here." Dark color burnished his cheekbones. "Bathroom. We can lock the door."

Robin was far enough gone to think that was a great idea. To heck with what his father would think if he came downstairs with perfect timing to see the two of them stepping out of the bathroom with wild hair, swollen lips and clothing not quite fastened right.

Seth carried her again. She squirmed against him until he was swearing under his breath. He had her pants off within about five seconds of them reaching the tiny half bath.

"Lock," she mumbled.

"What?" The blue of his eyes was molten. "Oh. Yeah."

He pushed the little button, picked her up and planted her butt on the edge of the vanity top. It didn't even cross her mind that the edge of the sink didn't make for comfortable seating. She was too busy easing down the zipper to free him.

He backed away long enough to sheath himself and then without any preamble drove inside her. When she cried out, Seth stifled the sound by covering her mouth with his. He moved fast and hard, giving her exactly what she seemed to need. Tender and slow was for another time.

Her body imploded. Seth followed, the throbbing almost setting her off again.

Finally, his head dropped forward to rest on her shoulder. He was shaking.

It took them a few minutes to get dressed, but once they had they went to the living room and cuddled on the sofa.

"Sorry," he murmured. "It's awkward sharing the house with a parent. I've been trying to keep my distance from you. I haven't been doing so well with it, though."

"No." Robin rubbed her cheek on his shirt. "Me, either."

They lapsed into a contented silence. It had to be five minutes before Seth said, "Earlier, when you asked, Dad and I were talking about my idea of putting a woman cop in your house."

Robin pulled away, incredulous. "You think Richard's stupid? He'll know I'd never go back there."

"No, I don't think he'd fall for that, but if

I can sneak you away again and the woman cop moves in *here...*"

"What, you're going to abandon your father to face another attack?"

"I intend to send him with you. I'll stay here."

No wonder they'd been arguing. Hadn't Seth known how insulted his father would be?

"I hate that idea," she said fiercely.

His arm tightened around her. "I know."

"He found us here." The certainty had the weight of dread. "He may be back in Seattle, but somebody has to be watching. Richard will find us wherever we go."

"I'd suspect his PI saw my name linked to the investigation and took a look at my house and then my father's, except..."

She had no trouble finishing his sentence. "Detectives don't take their work home with them." Thinking about that, she scooted far enough away to let her really study him. "Why did you?"

"You know why."

"Because you were attracted to me?"

She'd swear she saw a smile in his eyes that hadn't touched his mouth.

"Because I knew you were going to take off. Because with Jacob you were especially vulnerable. Because you looked too much like a dead woman." Now the smile reached his lips. "Because I felt a lot more than lust from the beginning."

Robin made herself ask. "Are you sorry?"

"No." His big hand closed gently over hers. "Never. I'd have been haunted by you for a long time if you'd succeeded in disappearing."

"I...wouldn't have forgotten you, either." She looked away for a moment. "I knew you'd be hurt when you found we were gone," she admitted.

"You were right," he said quietly, eyes intent on her face. "I would have been."

She would always feel guilt about Andrea, but she knew how lucky she and Jacob were that Seth had been the detective in charge of the investigation. He seemed willing to take any risk for them. Robin thought he'd risk a whole lot for any vulnerable woman or child. But...if his dad was right, he'd never brought one home before.

It still boggled her mind that she was able to trust him so absolutely. She could probably thank her father for that. Even at the worst with Richard, she hadn't forgotten that steady, kind men did exist.

"Do you think Richard has given up? That...he's hoping you'll decide it wasn't him who broke in here and shot your dad?"

His face hardened. "No." He hesitated as if not sure he wanted to say this, but chose to go on. "I think he's setting us up."

"I can't imagine he'd be satisfied by killing me secondhand," she argued again. And yet... She tried to get into her ex-husband's head. "I don't know," she finally admitted. "I can also picture how smug he'd feel if the police came to talk to him. He could be laughing inside." She formed an expression of dismay and concern. "'Detective, I was dining with the mayor last night. A dozen people can vouch that I was there. I don't understand what you think I can tell you.'"

"He'd be home free, except for one little problem."

"The man he'd paid to do his dirty work."

Sounding grim, Seth said, "But Brad McCormick's disappearance suggests your ex-husband knows how to solve that kind of problem."

Robin couldn't believe she was having this kind of conversation about her own, hypothetical murder. Seth didn't seem to be taking it in stride, either, thank goodness; he looked more disturbed than she felt.

"The thing is," she said slowly, "I still think he'd get a big charge out of killing me himself. I could never tell if he actually *enjoyed* hurting me, but..."

Seth's big body jerked.

She swallowed and finished, "There'd be something in his attitude afterward."

His face set with cold determination. "Let me just say that if I'm going to have a shoot-out with anyone, I'd just as soon it was him."

A miniflashback rattled her. "One shoot-out was enough, thank you. If only we could prove he was here and you could get a warrant for his guns."

"We've flashed photos at rental-car companies. Cops in half a dozen jurisdictions have helped. We've even tried ones in Vancouver." The city was across the Columbia River from Portland, which put it in Washington State. "Unfortunately, given that he owns a small plane, your ex can land at a private field anywhere. Now, after all his effort to assure us he's an extremely busy man who couldn't possibly get away, he'll have a plan to make the round-trip as fast as possible."

"Lovely thought." She was hugging herself again.

Seth noticed, too. He lifted his arm, and she all but dived into his embrace.

"Damn, I wish I could sleep with you tonight."

Robin thought that this time he wasn't even

thinking about sex. She pressed a kiss to his throat. "Me, too," she whispered.

NOT LONG AFTER breakfast the next morning, Robin turned to Seth. "Can you do a grocery run? We really need some basics."

He frowned but gave a grudging nod. He obviously didn't want to leave, but the couple of local grocery stores didn't deliver. "Make a list and I'll go."

"I already have a list. Just give me a minute to make sure I haven't forgotten anything."

Two minutes later, he was gone after a few quiet words with his father.

Michael had a holster on his belt now to carry his gun. Most of the time, Seth wore a long-sleeve shirt with the tails loose to hide his service pistol. Michael wasn't bothering. Robin knew that by now she ought to be used to seeing men openly carrying lethal weapons even to the bathroom or to get a snack out of the refrigerator, but she hadn't totally adjusted. Every time Richard had opened his huge gun safe and insisted she admire his collection, she'd felt queasy. There was a reason why she'd closed her eyes when he made her try target shooting.

And yet here she was now, being guarded by armed men. And glad of them, if a little unsettled.

Michael currently sat at the kitchen table, the newspaper open in front of him. He appeared to be glaring at the new exterior door.

"Damn kid thinks he can tell his old man what to do," he growled.

"He's scared for us," Robin reminded him.

"Mommy?" Jacob had been sitting on the floor playing with his simple wood puzzles, but now he got up and tugged at her pant leg. "Potty."

"Then let's go." Since his kiddy seat was upstairs, she bent to pick him up.

A dark shadow slid across one of the kitchen windows covered by a sheer roller shade.

Chapter Fifteen

Seth's foot kept easing from the accelerator. Apprehension rode him. He shouldn't have left the house. Left Robin, Jacob and his dad.

If he hustled, he could get to town, do the shopping and be back in not much over half an hour. That wasn't very long to be away. They had to eat.

He watched his rearview mirror, checked his phone. If anything went wrong, Dad or Robin would call.

He was lucky this road was so little traveled. If it carried much traffic at all, cars would be piling up behind him.

When his phone rang, Seth pulled to the shoulder. Sergeant Hammond, he saw as he answered.

"We've lost him," Hammond said without preamble. "Winstead is scheduled to be a speaker at a Rotary Club dinner tonight, but that gives him plenty of time to get down there and back. I just called Boeing Field. He didn't file a flight plan—rarely does, according to the woman I spoke to—but he did fly out several hours ago."

"He could already be here." *And I just left my family unprotected.*

"Where are *you*?" the sergeant asked.

"Not where I should be," Seth said, panic making it hard to get the words out. He ended the call, dropped his phone on the seat and wrenched the steering wheel to make a U-turn. Then he slammed his foot down on the accelerator.

ROBIN FROZE, HANDS outstretched but not yet touching Jacob. Could she have imagined what she thought she saw?

No.

Mouth dry, she whispered, "Michael."

He swiveled toward her, going to alert just from what he'd heard in her voice.

"Someone's outside."

He rose soundlessly, pulled his gun and held it in a two-handed grip with the barrel pointing down. He reached her in a couple of strides. "You two upstairs."

She picked up her son and made sure he was looking at her when she touched her finger to her lips. "Shh."

He let out a kind of squeak and burrowed into her.

"Come with us," she whispered.

Michael nodded.

Robin placed each foot as carefully as she could. The hall felt like a refuge until she saw the raw holes in the wallboard they hadn't yet repaired.

She looked back to see Michael with his back to her, his gaze sweeping the house. She crept up the stairs rather than racing the way she wanted to. *Get Jacob in the bathtub. Call Seth and then 9-1-1.*

Or the other way around?

He might not have gotten all the way to town. Robin's thoughts had fragmented, leaving her with no idea how long it had been since he left.

She was shaking by the time she bent over to lay Jacob down in the cast-iron tub.

"No!" he cried. "Don't go, Mommy! Stay!"

She clamped a hand over his mouth. "Shh, shh, shh."

His teeth chattered under her palm. Freckles stood out on his face like dots made by a permanent marker. The terrible fear in his eyes undid her.

Hearing the squeak of a floorboard, she

spun, almost falling over. It was Michael, right outside the bathroom.

"Got your phone?" he asked quietly.

Her head bobbed as she slid it from her pocket. "I'll call. But…what if there's nobody here?"

"Better safe."

Than sorry. Of course he was right.

Seth answered after one ring, his voice tense. "Robin?"

"We think… *I* think I saw someone right outside. We…we're upstairs."

"Dad with you?"

"Yes."

"I'm on my way back. I'll be there in about two minutes."

From town?

"Hammond called. Winstead took off in his plane hours ago."

Oh.

Glass shattered downstairs. Jacob let out a cry and Robin jumped.

"He just broke a window."

"Lock yourself in the bathroom again," Seth demanded.

"But I can't leave your dad—"

"Do it." That implacable note in his voice demanded obedience. "I'm almost there."

She knew the call had been dropped, but said, "Seth?" anyway.

Silence.

SETH GOT ON the radio to demand backup. He'd have asked for SWAT except the team wouldn't make it out here in time to do any good. If he was lucky, another unit might be nearby.

That piece of scum had already been on the property watching the house, waiting until the inhabitants gave him an opening. This time, by God, he wouldn't be driving away so he could take the podium in front of a bunch of businessmen to impress them with his ideas, passion for the underdogs, sharp sense of humor and make it seem impossible he was a predator with blood on his hands.

Seth's truck crested the hill on the two-lane country road at an unsafe speed, but he didn't so much as tap the brakes.

"CLOSE THE DOOR," Michael snapped. Bending slowly as if his joints hurt, he lowered himself to the floor. As Robin watched, he stretched out on his belly in the hall. That put him in a good position to see anyone coming up those stairs before they saw him. Only then he groaned and his face twisted as he tried to stretch his arms out in front of him with the gun pointed straight ahead.

Robin's stomach cramped painfully. He'd been wounded in his right shoulder. She'd known his mobility was hampered. *Could* he squeeze the trigger?

She crawled out. "Let me—"

He shot her an angry glance. "Get back in there. I can do this."

"Do you have another gun?" she whispered.

He stared fixedly at the empty space above the staircase. "Gun safe in my closet. There's a backup." He reeled off a combination.

She looked back at the bathtub, unable to see Jacob without standing all the way up. This was how it would feel to be ripped in half. Go. Stay.

No. She couldn't crouch helpless in the bathroom while a wounded man in his sixties died to defend her.

Still bent over, she ran for the master bedroom.

A sudden, furious barrage of gunfire deafened her. Crying out, she dropped to the carpeted floor. That sounded like half a dozen guns. Richard hadn't come alone this time.

In the sudden silence, she crawled the rest of the way into the closet, twirled the dial with a shaking hand and took out the pistol she recognized right away as a revolver.

She pushed herself to her feet and hurried to the doorway, setting her back to the door as she'd seen actors do in action shows on TV, edging over to see the hall.

Michael hadn't moved. The wallboard and ceiling above him were shredded, but from the back he appeared unhurt and alert. With a moan, Robin got down and crawled fast toward him and her terrified son.

HALF A MILE. Quarter of a mile. Seth's truck rocked and swerved as he made the turn into the driveway. He swore at the sudden realization that he wasn't wearing his vest.

God, had Dad been wearing the one Seth had borrowed for him?

That's when he heard a volley of gunfire. So many shots, it was like approaching an outdoor gun range.

He wouldn't accept that he was too late.

Sunlight glinted off windows that appeared unbroken across the front of the house. Hoping to draw the gunman or gunmen out of the house, he skidded to a stop in his usual parking place. At a fleeting glance, he saw neither movement nor any damage here, either.

Even as he shut down the engine, Seth bent

over to get out, intent on shielding behind the door he'd just opened. He hadn't quite made it when the windows in the truck exploded simultaneously and he fell the rest of the way to the packed gravel.

Teeth clenched, he scrambled behind the rear bumper, forcing himself to regroup. It had been a while since he'd heard or seen what a semiautomatic assault rifle could do.

Crouching behind the truck, he lifted the hatch and grabbed his Kevlar vest.

In the act of reaching for a tab on the vest, he saw something that made him pause. Dark splotches on the gravel. Oh, hell. Blood soaked his shirtsleeve and dripped from his hand. One of those bullets had found him, and he hadn't even felt it. Still didn't feel it. He wiped blood off his hand on his jeans and finished closing the Velcro.

Judging from the earlier blast, Winstead had shot his way into the house. Did he already have Jacob? Seth shook his head. The only possible way that bastard could have gotten his hands on the boy they all loved was by killing the two adults in the house. They'd made it upstairs, he knew that. He wouldn't believe they were dead.

He knew from experience that the pain would hit suddenly. He hoped it held off and didn't blindside him. His Glock held in firing position, he crept along the passenger side of his truck, careful not to give away his position with a crunch of gravel. Being up against an assault rifle didn't intimidate him. He needed only one shot—the right shot.

ROBIN HAD REACHED Michael and the bathroom door when a second explosion of gunfire began. She dropped to the floor again, and saw Michael try to pancake himself. Since shreds of wallboard didn't fly, she worked out that the shots weren't here in the house.

"Damn it," Michael ground out. "I'll bet Seth just got here."

Suddenly sick, she felt sure Seth had driven up openly in an attempt to draw Richard's attention. If he'd died in the hail of bullets—

Robin wiped a wet cheek. "It sounds like Richard brought an army. Why would he do that?"

Michael took his gaze off the head of the stairs for a fleeting instant. "I don't think he did. Sounds like an assault rifle to me."

Feeling even sicker, Robin could only think, *Of course.* After reading about school shootings where teenagers had gotten their hands on an AR-15 or the like, Robin had been horrified when she first saw the two Richard owned. She asked why he had them and he'd said, *Because I can.* Imagine what the members of the Seattle city council would think if they knew he owned guns at all, far less the most lethal of them. That was Richard in a nutshell: the facade of being a compassionate man, an activist, that he wore like the too-thin crust of cooling lava over the deadly red-hot flow beneath.

"What can we do?" she whispered.

Michael shook his head. "Nothing."

So she crouched in the doorway to the bathroom, sweaty hands gripping the gun. And waited.

SETH FLATTENED HIMSELF on the ground beside the front fender of the truck. He'd see legs and feet if that piece of scum appeared around the corner of the house. Winstead might be a crack shot, but he hadn't served in the military or had police training and experience. From the way Seth had barreled up to the house, Winstead must know other cops would be on the way. His window of opportunity was closing. He'd want to be sure Seth was dead before he resumed the attack indoors. Even if he was capable of patience, he couldn't afford it.

Unless he assumed Seth was down.

Or unless he really did already have Jacob

and was even now fleeing through the woods to wherever he'd left his car. That ugly possibility and the complete silence felt like an itch Seth couldn't scratch.

His gut said he was doing the right thing. But a single glance told him he was bleeding like a stuck pig.

Another burst of gunfire came from inside the house. Seth jumped to his feet and ran.

MICHAEL ROLLED, GROANING. Blood. New blood.

"If you want the kid to survive," Richard called up the stairs, arrogance in his voice, "you won't shoot. You'll let me come up and take my son. Too late for *yours*. He's dead, and you're outgunned."

No!

In horror, Robin saw that during the fusillade, Michael had dropped his pistol. He fumbled to pick it up, but he couldn't seem to close his fingers. In desperation, he reached for it with his left hand.

The devastation of knowing that Seth was dead felt like hearing the bone-rattling crack of thunder right above her when she was utterly exposed in the open, waiting for the lightning bolt. What Richard couldn't know was that her unacknowledged grief served as fuel to make her hate burn even hotter.

Robin rose to her feet slowly, still unable to see Richard. She braced her feet the way he had taught her. Gripped the gun with both hands, finger resting on the trigger. *Aim low*, she told herself, almost coldly, *assume there'll be some kick*.

There was the top of a blue baseball cap.

One more step, she begged him silently.

He took it, their eyes met…and from the foot of the stairs came a harsh command.

"Drop the gun! Now!"

Richard whirled, rifle still held in firing position.

She pulled the trigger, heard the *crack* of other shots, and saw Richard fall forward and disappear. Three loud thuds had to be his body bouncing down the stairs.

"Robin?" Seth called, sounding frantic. "Dad? I'm coming up."

Her arms lost all strength and sagged so that the gun pointed at the floor. "We're here," she managed to say. "We're okay." And she crouched to set the handgun down.

Just as Seth appeared, his face hard and expressing the terror he had felt, she heard a siren in the distance.

ABOUT READY TO abandon Michael's old pickup in the middle of one of the rows of parked cars at the hospital, and who cared if it got towed, Robin finally spotted an open slot. She pulled in, jumped out and ran for the emergency room entrance.

They hadn't let her go to the hospital with Seth and Michael. "They" being responding law enforcement that included a couple of different uniforms and ranks from chief to deputy. She wasn't injured, so they expected her to walk them all through what happened. Anyway, they told her she wouldn't be allowed to take a child Jacob's age into a recovery room or to visit either man if they were put in intensive care or even moved to a room to spend the night.

Hanging on to her sanity by a fragile thread, she had told the whole story from beginning to end twice, and today's events half a dozen times. Interviewed in the living room, she'd still been aware of the flashes going off as a crime scene investigator photographed her ex-husband's body, sprawled over the bottom steps, booted feet up, head down.

She would never forget the sight of the man she'd once married dead from multiple bullet holes. Although thank goodness for Seth, who had carried Jacob downstairs, making sure he didn't see even a blood splatter. Except, maybe, the blood dripping from Seth himself.

She still didn't know if her shot had killed Richard or hit the body armor he'd worn. Hers hadn't been the only shots fired, though. Seth had fired multiple times, she thought, and Michael at least once. Whichever of them had killed him, she didn't feel the teeniest bit of regret.

Iris had been glad to take Jacob once Robin had been allowed to leave. Now she hurried up to the receptionist.

"Seth Renner? The detective?"

"And you are?"

"Robin Hollis. I'm living with him and his father," she said simply. "The investigators held me up to take my account of what happened."

"Let me check."

Two minutes later, she returned. "Mr. Renner senior is still here in the ER, but Detective Renner was taken to surgery. I show him as being in recovery now."

Robin asked if she could see Michael, and was ushered through the double doors. She found a frantic man wearing his own pants and a hospital gown who insisted no one would tell him anything. They'd had to remove a large splinter—the four inches long kind—but felt most of his "discomfort" came from the previous wound. He'd been to X-ray and was now waiting to be taken for an MRI when all he wanted was to know how his son was.

With his blessings, she rushed to the surgical suite, where she had to wait for a maddening fifteen minutes before she was permitted to see Seth.

Half-sitting up in bed, he was crunching on ice chips. He looked both wonderful and awful, woozy, his skin pasty and his hair lank—but alive. Awake. His expression lightened the minute he saw her, and he reached out his good hand.

Robin latched onto it. "They removed a bullet?"

"No, just had to do some repair work," he said grumpily. "They didn't even have to use full anesthesia. I'm not in a daze, and I want out of here."

She leaned over and kissed his scratchy cheek. "Your father is just as crabby."

He demanded to know what had been happening, so she told him about the questioning, about taking Jacob to Iris's and what she knew about his father's condition.

Then he focused on her in that way he had. "Are you all right, Robin?"

Her smile turned tremulous, but she said, "Yes. It was horrible and scary, but…"

"It's all over."

"My knees keep wobbling, but at the same time I feel as if I can take a full breath for the first time in years. If you hadn't stopped me from taking off…"

"I did a lousy job protecting you." His voice was bleak, his eyes unflinching. "If Hammond hadn't called, I don't know whether I'd have turned around and gotten back in time."

"I thought you were dead." The memory was so vivid, for a fleeting moment he *was* dead. The memory of her shock and horror was that real. "I thought…" Her throat clogged.

"You believed him?" For all his postsurgery state and self-imposed guilt trip, Seth pulled a grin from somewhere. "No faith in me at all."

Cheeks wet, she leaned over to press her face to the white blanket over his chest. His heart beat strongly, his chest rose and fell. "I hope I killed him," she mumbled.

"No." He stroked her hair, his voice a rumble that was somehow also soft. "You saw plenty to give yourself years of nightmares. You don't need more on your conscience."

Impatient with herself, she wiped away tears and reared up. "Why would it be on my conscience? He intended to kill *us*, and then steal Jacob. Abuse him, hit him—" Robin choked on the rest. What would Richard have turned her sunny-natured child into? It didn't bear thinking about.

"Okay." Seth ran his knuckles over her jaw, his expression so tender her eyes burned again. "Have you called home yet?"

She stared at him. "What?"

"Bet your mother would like to hear from you. Your sister, too. They'll get to meet Jacob at last." Then he smiled crookedly, his eyes clearer than they'd been. "They can let the doctors know to schedule that surgery."

"I had to see you." Actually, the thought of calling home hadn't even crossed her mind yet. But if it had…she would still have raced right to the hospital.

Seth captured her hand again. Suddenly he looked uncertain. "You'll stay in Lookout, won't you? I mean, after you visit your family. You have to know I'm in love with you."

"I'm in love with you, too." Her vision was annoyingly blurry. "Damn it, you're turning me to mush."

"Good." This smile blazed with happiness. "C'mere." He tugged, and she went.

Normally Robin would have wondered how he could kiss like this with a cocktail of drugs still in his bloodstream and a heavily bandaged arm. As it was, all she could do was kiss him back. Starting gentle, they took the leap into passion. If he'd been in a private room, they might have gotten really serious, or as serious as his blood loss allowed. As it was… Robin broke away to rest her head against his shoulder.

His hand played in her hair, and his chest rose and fell with each breath. Robin felt impossibly young. No, that wasn't quite it, she decided, finally identifying a long unfamiliar emotion.

Hope.

Epilogue

On a sunny July afternoon, Robin's small family barbecued and celebrated in her mother's backyard. The sun shone, Mom's treasured roses bloomed brilliantly, Seth flipped burgers on the ancient Weber grill set up on the patio and Jacob had just collapsed in the shade after running in circles until he was too dizzy to stand.

Having refused help beyond Seth's contribution, Mom bustled in and out of the house carrying food and dishes. Her cheeks looked a little pinker than the warm day justified, possibly because Michael smiled every time he saw her.

Robin and Allie lay back comfortably in matching chaise lounges. Sunlight and shade flickered over them when the breeze moved the leaves of the flowering cherry tree. Robin wore a strapless sundress, Allie shorts and a polo shirt that hid her dialysis catheter and port, but let Robin see how frail her sister had become.

"You know I'm going to lose my best reading time," Allie commented lazily.

Robin turned her head to grin at her. "Dialysis was so relaxing?"

Allie laughed. "I just figure I should add a cloud so the silver lining isn't too dazzling."

The surgery was scheduled for tomorrow. By the end of the day, Robin would be short one kidney, and Allie would finally have a healthy, functioning one. Sometimes Robin still had trouble believing they'd gotten this far. And as she did every time she had that thought, she looked toward Seth. Her savior, her lover, her fiancé.

He'd asked to adopt Jacob, who would soon have a grandfather as well as a grandmother.

The smile he gave her was warm, sexy... and a promise.

He set down the plate of burgers on the table and raised his voice. "Come and get it."

Jacob leaped and ran straight to him. Seth scooped him up, gave him an exceptionally gentle airplane ride and plopped him into his booster seat.

Feeling as if she could float to the table like dandelion fluff, she instead rose to her feet and held out her hand for her sister's. "Enjoy this. I think you're about to find out if hospital food stinks as much as I hear it does."

Allie smiled with simple delight. "Small price to pay."

"You're right." They hugged, found their places at the picnic table and started to dish up.

* * * * *

Get 4 FREE REWARDS!

We'll send you 2 FREE Books <u>plus</u> 2 FREE Mystery Gifts.

Harlequin® Romantic Suspense books feature heart-racing sensuality and the promise of a sweeping romance set against the backdrop of suspense.

FREE Value Over **$20**

Get 4 FREE REWARDS!

We'll send you 2 FREE Books plus 2 FREE Mystery Gifts.

YES! Please send me 2 FREE Harlequin Presents® novels and my 2 FREE gifts (gifts are worth about $10 retail). After receiving them, if I don't wish to receive any more books, I can return the shipping statement marked "cancel." If I don't cancel, I will receive 6 brand-new novels every month and be billed just $4.55 each for the regular-print edition or $5.55 each for the larger-print edition in the U.S., or $5.49 each for the regular-print edition or $5.99 each for the larger-print edition in Canada. That's a savings of at least 11% off the cover price! It's quite a bargain! Shipping and handling is just 50¢ per book in the U.S. and 75¢ per book in Canada.* I understand that accepting the 2 free books and gifts places me under no obligation to buy anything. I can always return a shipment and cancel at any time. The free books and gifts are mine to keep no matter what I decide.

Choose one: ☐ **Harlequin Presents®**
Regular-Print
(106/306 HDN GMYX)

☐ **Harlequin Presents®**
Larger-Print
(176/376 HDN GMYX)

Name (please print)

Address   Apt. #

City   State/Province   Zip/Postal Code

Mail to the **Reader Service:**
IN U.S.A.: P.O. Box 1341, Buffalo, NY 14240-8531
IN CANADA: P.O. Box 603, Fort Erie, Ontario L2A 5X3

Want to try 2 free books from another series? Call 1-800-873-8635 or visit www.ReaderService.com.